I0689281

FIERCE GUARDIAN

Fire and Snow
Book Four

KHLOE WREN

Books by Khloe Wren

Fire and Snow:
Guardian's Heart
Noble Guardian
Guardian's Shadow
Fierce Guardian

Dragon Warriors:
Enchanting Eilagh
Binding Becky
Claiming Carina
Seducing Skye
Believing Binda

Jaguar Secrets:
Jaguar Secrets
FireStarter

Single Titles:
Fireworks
Tigers Are Forever
Bad Alpha Anthology
Scarred Perfection
Scandals: Zeck
Mirror Image Seduction

ISBN: 978-0-9945190-9-2

Cover Credits:
Photographer: John Mitchell
Model: John Quinlan
Digital Artist: Jay Aheer of Simply Defined Art

Editing Credits:
Editor: Carolyn Depew of Write Right
Proofreader: Ami Deason

Acknowledgements

As I poured my soul into this book, my family supported me. As usual when my beautiful and infinitely patient husband found me in tears at my computer, he handed me chocolate before walking away chuckling. (He never has understood my connection to fictional characters). While I'm lost in bookworld, he not only keeps the house running and us all fed, but he helps me thrash out plot issues too! Truly, he is my hero. To my girls, thank you for sharing Mummy with the world inside her head. To my parents, your continual unconditional love and support means the world to me.

To all my friends who helped me get back up each time I stumbled while writing this book. Becky McGraw, Ashley Martinez and Tamsin Baker you three especially.

Sandra, a huge shout out in thanks for helping me make Rachel sound more British. I love that we've managed to put the word 'shagging' in the book.

To cover model, John Quinlan. Thank you for being my friend, since meeting you three years ago, I'm proud to say Xander has taken on some of your personality.

To my editing team, Carolyn and Ami, I thank you for putting up with the nightmares my bad guys give you, and for helping me make this book all it could be.
xo
Khloe Wren

Biography

Khloe Wren grew up in the Adelaide Hills before her parents moved the family to country South Australia when she was a teen. It was there that Khloe followed her father's footsteps and joined the volunteer firefighting service at 18. A few years later, Khloe moved to Melbourne which unfortunately meant she had to give up firefighting but she's always missed it. After a few years living in the big city, she missed the fresh air and space of country living so returned to rural South Australia. Khloe currently lives in the Murraylands with her incredibly patient husband, two strong willed young daughters, an energetic dog and two curious cats.

Khloe has always loved big cats, especially Snow Leopards. So it seemed only natural that when she began writing her first novel after having major surgery that left her on bedrest for six months, that she chose these beautiful creatures as her first shifters.

Glossary

Alpha (of a Leap): The leader of the Leap.

Continental Leap: The Leap chosen to represent their continent at the Council of Alphas. Each of the seven continents has a Continental Leap.

Council of Alphas: The Alpha of each Continental Leap form the Council of Alphas. It is their job to oversee all aspects of shifter life.

Dream Bonding: After the female turns twenty-one, shifter pairs can pull each other into a dream. Useful for when mates are apart from each other.

Chaton: French for kitten.

Comet Shifters: Those shifters newly created from Halley's Comet's passing of Earth.

David Jones: Large department store.

Firie/Firies/Firie's: Nickname for a firefighter

Halley's Comet: When the shifters were first created. Halley's Comet passed as the magic was welded. Now, every seventy-five years when the comet passes over Earth, a new pair of shifters is conceived on each continent.

Jaws of Life: Apparatus Firefighters use to cut open crashed vehicles in order to save the occupants

Leap: Leap is the name given to a group of Snow Leopards.

Lost Ones: Shifters who are not part of a Leap and often don't know of their heritage. Lost Ones are often alone and scared of what they are, not understanding there are others like them.

Maman: French for Mum/Mom

Marking, The: After mating, the couple mark each other with permanent scratch marks to show their claim on the other. The mark looks like four wide scratch marks that reveal Snow Leopard spots beneath.

Mating: The process a couple goes through to bind themselves together for life. Mating forms an unbreakable bond.

Ma chère: French endearment, my dear.

Mon amour: French endearment, my love.

Petit fille: French for little girl/daughter

Search, The: On of the Council of Alphas' main purposes is to go looking for Lost Ones and Comet Shifters.

Shifter Magic: Because shifters were created with magic, they hold a low level of magic which they can weld on occasion.

Tibetan Monks: Tibetan Monks are the ones who originally cast the magic to bind a man and a Snow Leopard together.

Trigger: Trigger Corporation is the enemy to the shifters.

Ute: Similar to an American Pickup Truck

Widow Mate: Mate of a shifter who has died. Once their mate dies, they are free to find love again if they choose to.

Dedication

To anyone suffering, this storm is only part of your
journey, not your final destination. Keep fighting.

Author's Note

This book is extremely close to my heart. I've personally
lived through abuse similar to what Rachel suffers.
Emotional and mental abuse is extremely damaging, it
tears you down until you feel you have nothing left.
Often, it happens so slowly you don't realize it's
happened. One day something happens that makes you
sit back and say to yourself 'whoa, how did I get here?'

If you're suffering abuse, there's help out there. Search
for it, never stop fighting for yourself. The best decision I
ever made was to break free. Eleven years later, I have a
beautiful loving husband and two wonderful daughters.
They are worth every moment I had to fight.

Prologue

Breath rushed from Xander's lungs, as though he'd been sucker punched, when he looked into the hazel eyes of the woman behind the bar as she focused her attention on his Alpha, Jake. When he'd agreed to join Jake, Dominic, Sean, Jordan and Joel on this little expedition down to Hobart to investigate if Classic Convicts was being run by their enemy, Trigger, he'd never expected to run into his mate. As all snow leopard shifter males did, Xander had been dreaming of this woman since she'd turned twenty-one, which had been the ninth of March 2007. For more than five years Xander had seen her every time he laid down to sleep at night. His fingers twitched as he remembered how silky her chocolate brown hair was. In his dreams, it hadn't ever been slicked up into a mohawk like the one she currently wore.

"So, what can I get you boys?"

He bit his cheek to stop a groan escaping. The lilt of her British accent was so much more potent in real life. Xander now knew for sure that Mate Dreams were a watered down version of the real thing. She was certainly more stunning to look at in real life than she'd been in his nightly visions.

"A jug of beer and six glasses. Thanks love."

"Name's Rachel, not love, and that'll be eighteen dollars, thanks."

His lips curled into a smirk at his mate's feisty response to Jake's endearment as he rolled her name around in his mind, *Rachel*. He held himself completely motionless as he tracked her movements. She leaned down to grab an empty jug and his dick stiffened when he caught a glimpse of her lace-covered breasts down her shirt. With ease, she filled Jake's order and had the jug and six glasses sitting on the mat. With her hand still wrapped around the final glass, she finally looked away from what she was doing to run her gaze over them. Xander barely repressed a growl as she checked out his leap brothers. He forced his lungs to function. Of course she was going to look. Even as a heterosexual male, Xander had to admit shifter males were a good looking breed. Jake's quiet chuckle filled the air a moment before Rachel's gaze landed on him, and she froze as her breath hitched.

Oh yeah, baby girl. You feel it don't you? You're mine.

He sensed the others looking at him but he didn't budge. He opened his mouth to speak but was cut off by Jake as he thanked Rachel, then gathered the jug of beer. The Alpha of their leap then all but shoved Xander away from his mate. Xander detested being ordered around and turned his angry gaze on Jake, but stopped short when he saw the seriousness in the older man's eyes. Something was up.

Jake was highly empathic and Xander was certain the man knew Rachel was his mate by the emotions that he'd been radiating since first seeing her. With a frown he turned on his heel and joined his leap brothers as they moved to a booth in the rear of the bar. As soon as they all sat down Xander turned on Jake.

"That's my mate. Why'd you pull me away?"

"You didn't see her left hand?"

Left hand? His body tensed at what he feared Jake was about to tell him.

"Didn't look, it was her face I was watching."

"Looks like she's engaged, son."

"Fuck."

Instinctively his gaze returned to his mate and a growl rolled out of his mouth as he fought down the desire to kill the man dumb enough to touch what was his. *She's meant for me.* The possessive thought repeated on a loop in his mind as he watched a male manhandle his mate.

"Can you hear what he's saying to her, Xander?"

Like Jake, Xander was one of the few shifters who'd been born with a special skill. While Jake could pick up on others' emotions, feeling them as if they were his own, Xander had enhanced hearing. Generally speaking, he could hear with better clarity and at further distances than other shifters. But what came in really handy, especially at times like this, was that he could focus it. It had taken him years to perfect how to use this particular skill but he could now easily concentrate on a conversation, even if it was a distance away from him, blocking out all other noises and being able to hear it as if he was standing next to the one talking.

Tuning out everything else in the bar, he honed in on Rachel and the bastard with her.

"Don't lie to me, pet. I was watching the cameras."

"Really Rocco? Spying on me? And I thought you were snowed under with work."

"Stop trying to change the subject, Rachel. I saw how you looked at him. What? You tired of me or something? Is the fact I've always provided for you, given you a job and a home, made it so you can stay in Australia, not enough suddenly?"

"Oh, seriously? You're getting all macho because I *looked* at a man? I'm not blind and those men are good looking. You know full well I'd never cheat on you."

"I know, beautiful. You're mine and I get jealous, I can't help it. I know how gorgeous you are and know full well other men would take you from me in a heartbeat if I'm not careful."

Taking a deep breath Xander released his focus and let the rest of the bar's sounds enter his mind. He'd heard all he could take for now. The guy was an asshole, and he obviously had no respect or trust in Rachel.

"Yeah, I can hear the bastard. He didn't like the way she looked at me. Prick was watching her on the surveillance cameras."

Xander's muscles relaxed a little when Jake's warm palm squeezed his shoulder. "You can't go over and take her. I wish you could, but that's not how it works. She saw you, sensed something between you. Take it slow with her and you'll win her over. Engaged isn't married and if that's the owner of her ring — well, she doesn't exactly look real happy with him now, does she?"

"No, she isn't. I saw the look in her eyes and it was as far from happy as you get."

Even though he wasn't zoned in on Rachel anymore he could still catch some of the conversation and he tensed with fury at what he just heard.

"Fuck, the pervert sitting at the bar asked him why Rachel isn't on next door. Apparently she'll be out over there real soon."

Intense rage shuddered through his body when Rocco palmed Rachel's breast before he told her to go get ready. When he released his hold, Rachel hurried away, but not quickly enough to miss Rocco's hand slapping her ass. How dare he lay a hand on his mate? A deep, dangerous growl left his throat as he pictured all the brutal things he wanted to do to that man. When she was out of sight he swung his gaze back to Jake.

"Just told her to go get changed. We need to go next door. If that asshole puts her up on stage, I'm taking her."

The older man sighed and took a swig of his beer before he spoke.

"We've got your back, son."

Xander's stomach churned as he heard Rocco tell the other guy how good Rachel was on her knees. He lifted his glass and drained his beer before he slammed the thing down on the table.

"I'm out of here, I can't listen to him talk about my mate like he is. Fucking asshole."

As he moved to slide from the booth Jake stopped him.

"Xander, it's too early to go next door. Especially if he's noticed her watching you. Look at the tattoo on his neck. He's a Trigger. My guess would be that's Rocco Ferri, the owner. Let's just chill here for a little and see what other information we can pick up on in regard to Triggers, then we'll head on over to HoHaven. Rachel has to get changed before she'll be over there, so we have a little time."

Xander vibrated with his frustration. Dammit, but Jake had a point. He stared hard into Jake's face as he spoke.

"I don't like this, Jake. Every instinct I have is screaming for me to go get her. But I'm not stupid. Those few Triggers who survived last week could be here and if they see us and see me start something with her, they're going to know who she is to me, and that won't end well for her. That said, if she's on that damn stage when we go in there, I won't be able to stop myself. We clear?"

"Clear as day, son."

Heat scorched Rachel's cheeks as she scrambled down the stairs to where she'd left her bag in the waitress' change room. Rocco embarrassing her was nothing new, just as his possessive caveman side wasn't either. She hated that it still got to her. You'd think after, what—sixteen months—she'd be done reacting to his antics. Mind you, she'd also thought he'd cut the jealousy bullshit by now too. Those men were all hot. Like she wasn't going to have a look? Didn't mean she was going to touch. And it wasn't like Rocco didn't spend all night, every night, watching women strip. He was surrounded by good looking female flesh every day! Most nights it was only the drunken regulars in the Classic Convict and they were nothing to look at. All most of them wanted to know was when she'd be on the stage at HoHaven instead of behind the bar.

"When hell freezes over, that's when."

Rachel didn't have body issues or anything. She simply didn't want to be spank-bank fodder for a bunch of wankers who thought leering at women they don't know while they toss money at her was a good way to spend their night and hard earned money.

Reaching her locker, she quickly stripped off the Classic Convicts shirt and pulled on a HoHaven one. The shirts were skin-tight with a very low V-neck. If she'd been planning on going out clubbing with her friends, she'd have loved the fit. It showcased her C cup breasts and tucked in waist perfectly. The dark denim jeans hid not only any drink spills, but her wide hips and fleshy butt. It was a simple uniform that worked well. She matched it with Doc Martin boots, which she argued with Rocco over at least twice a week. He wanted her in fuck-me-heels, she didn't want broken ankles. She didn't bother fighting him on many things, it was just so much simpler to do things his way most of the time. But she wouldn't give in on this. If he wanted her working long hours on her feet, he had to deal with her choice in footwear.

A quick glance in the mirror to check that her mohawk

and makeup survived her shirt change had her reaching for her lipstick. Of all the things that set Rocco off, having her out in public without full makeup was the quickest. She sighed as she pressed her lips together. She probably shouldn't give in to his demands so much. But she didn't have anywhere else to go and being with him kept her in Australia. She'd never been able to settle in the UK, but here Down Under she fit right in with the laid back lifestyle.

An image of one of the men filled her mind. He'd been tall, at least six feet six, with a clean shaven head and a chiseled jaw line she could run her tongue along. Yeah, Rachel would bet a bloke like that could more than take care of a female. Maybe it was time to leave. Although, if she left Rocco and Classic Convicts it would kill her current Visa. Could she do it? Go back to England and settle down like her parents wanted her to? She shuddered. She might have finished the apprenticeship they'd set up for her at the posh exclusive restaurant Enlighten in the heart of London, but she'd never intended to stay there.

Strangely, they hadn't been against her plans to backpack around Australia for a year. Of course, they'd been mortified when she'd rung nine months in to tell them she'd met a man and was going to stay Down Under indefinitely. Thankfully, they'd never found out she worked the bar in a strip club. Rachel thought her mother may just pass out at the very idea of a strip club, let alone her precious only daughter working in one.

With the realization that she wouldn't be moving on to

greener pastures any time soon, Rachel headed out of the waitress' change room and quickly made her way past the strippers' change room, before making it to the bar area of HoHaven. The working girls were never nice to her, not that Rachel cared. Silly tarts were constantly throwing themselves at Rocco, thinking it would get them preferential treatment. She scoffed. Like hell it would. He'd promised her from the beginning that he never sampled the goods. That he wouldn't cheat on her.

Grabbing a fresh black apron from the stack by the entry, she tied it around her waist and made her way behind the bar to start serving drinks. There weren't any girls on the stage yet, so the few early arrivals were at the bar waiting for their drinks already. With quick efficacy she got the first round served and then the door from Classic Convicts opened and the group from earlier came in. Her heart sank. Guess they were like every other man on the planet—happy to pay good money simply to see a girl shake her bare ass. She might realize she'd never have anything with the bald giant, but in her imagination, she'd wanted him to be better than this.

"Hey dollface, what's such a pretty face doing behind the bar? You gonna take that shirt off for us and serve us topless while you shake those titties?"

She sneered at the drunk wanker and snapped at him.

"I'm here to serve drinks, not dance. You want to watch women taking their clothes off, turn your attention toward the stage, because I sure as fuck am not stripping back here for your, or anyone else's, entertainment."

She normally had more patience to deal with the idiots that came in every night, but tonight she couldn't muster it. For some reason, that one man, whose name she didn't even know, was affecting her on a soul-deep level that she wasn't entirely comfortable with. She glanced over at his table with a frown. Who the hell was he? Whoever he was, he didn't look comfortable and winced every time the bass heavy music thumped. The side door clicked open and Rachel made sure she was busy sorting out shit behind the bar. No way was she in the mood for more of Rocco's jealousy if he noticed her watching other men again.

Xander's skin itched as he fought against his instincts that demanded he take his mate and claim her. He glared at the door to HoHaven. Red leather with brass studs, he supposed it was meant to look luxurious. However, the big guy standing next to it with his bulging arms crossed over his broad chest ruined any attempt to make it look classy. The man was dressed well enough with a tight black t-shirt and dress pants, but the expression on his face made it clear he was nothing but a thug. Xander was beginning to understand Rocco was surrounded by nothing but sleaze-balls. How the hell had Rachel come to be caught up with him?

Xander growled under his breath, cursing himself for not going in search of her sooner. His parents had always told him to have patience and allow fate to decide when he met his mate. They'd assured him that shifters always found their mate when they needed each other the most.

Xander admitted, at least to himself, the other reason he'd not gone looking for her. About a year after he'd first dreamed of Rachel, he'd heard her voice and knew instantly her accent was British. He'd never been to England and had no idea where to start searching for her if he went. He was sure Jake could line up someone in a leap over there to assist him, but that would only help if she was one of them. The fact she was engaged to a Trigger had Xander thinking that she was most likely fully human.

Xander rolled his shoulders in an attempt to ease his tension. He glanced around the bar, taking in what the other patrons were doing. He looked at the faces of all the men, looking for Triggers they'd fought against at the farmhouse months ago.

"Oi, Rocco. Who's on stage tonight?"

The older man still sitting at the bar caught his attention as he spoke to Rocco. Xander honed his hearing in on the conversation.

"Full bill of girls tonight."

"Don't jerk me around, Rocco. You know what I'm asking."

Rocco laughed. "Yes, your favorite is up later. I'd be fool to not put Bella Diamond up on center stage. Woman pulls every dime from the crowd when she's on."

"Pity you can't convince her to work seven nights a week."

"Well, while she's pulling in what she is, she doesn't need to. Thursday through to Sunday is all we both need to make enough dough from her hot little body."

The older man sighed, "And what a body it is. Lucky bastard."

"That I am, buddy. That I am. Speaking of which, I'd better go check on things. I'll see you in there later."

Xander turned to watch as Rocco left the bar and headed over to the red door.

"What was that about, son?"

Jake's serious tone brought his attention away from the bar's owner.

"The club's apparent favorite stripper 'Bella Diamond' is going to be on stage tonight. The way Rocco and that sleaze spoke of her, has me thinking Rocco's sleeping with this stripper."

"So you think it might be Rachel?"

Xander clenched his jaw tight as fury raced through him. He couldn't speak, so he nodded at his Alpha. Jake frowned at him for a moment before he spoke.

"Okay, let's go in then. We all know the score. Try to not cause any trouble. We need to learn more about everyone involved here before we make any moves, so if we see any of the Triggers from the fight, we're out of here. Understand?"

He took a deep breath and focused on calming his emotions.

"I'll do my best, Jake. But I was serious when I told you I'd take her if he puts her on stage."

Jake sighed but didn't say a word as he moved out of the booth and headed over toward HoHaven. Xander allowed Jake to take the lead and speak to the thug guarding the door.

"Haven't seen you blokes before."

"Yeah, we wanted to try somewhere new tonight. So, what's the go?"

"Ten-dollar cover charge, twenty if you want to sit at the stage. There's rooms for private dances, or if you don't mind being watched, you can use one of the booths along the back wall." Xander bristled as the thug paused to run his gaze over each of them. "Rules are simple. So long as you keep buying drinks and tipping the girls, you won't have any issues. Start causing trouble, you'll get tossed out on your asses and banned."

"Fair enough."

Jake pulled his wallet free and handed the guy enough to cover all of them.

"We'll just hang back tonight. Maybe next time we'll get front row seats."

With a nod the door opened and Xander held his breath as he struggled to maintain his composed expression. He didn't want to tip off this thug to his emotional state, because if he found Rachel on that stage, he would redefine this idiot's definition of what trouble was. Once they passed the entrance, they faced a dimly lit staircase leading down.

"Guess it's in the basement. How classy."

Xander had to agree with Sean. The black peeling paint on the walls didn't inspire confidence in the quality of the place either.

"Let's get this over with."

As he spoke, Xander moved past the others to take the lead. The sooner they got in, the sooner they could leave. He didn't slow his stride as he pushed through the thick red curtain at the base of the stairs. Instantly the muted thumping music became intense. Xander winced as it assaulted his sensitive ears. He'd never liked eighties rock anthems. Damn, he wasn't going to be able to take this for long. He wished he'd brought earplugs with him.

"Dad, we have to leave. Xander's not doing so well."

Xander shook his head at Dominic. "I'm not leaving until I find out if Rachel is on that fucking stage."

The song finished and Xander closed his eyes a moment in gratitude. The next song started slow, LL Cool's "Doin' It". This he could handle. He strode over to a booth along the back wall and settled against the padded seat. The others followed his lead and a moment later a pretty waitress wearing a sparkly silver mini skirt and a tight black tank top that left her belly bare approached them. Xander let the others worry about drinks as he began to scan the club. It was relatively early, so there were only about a dozen men here. He didn't recognize any of them as Trigger. He then turned his attention to the stage. It was in the shape of a T, with three poles along the back then another one at the end of the catwalk. All four were being put to good use by women who looked nothing like Rachel. He exhaled slowly, suppressing his relief for the moment. He couldn't be certain she wouldn't be on stage later.

"I'm here to serve drinks, not dance. You want to watch women taking their clothes off, turn your attention toward the stage, because I sure as fuck am not stripping back here for your, or anyone else's, entertainment."

With a grin he turned toward the bar. He recognized her voice and he adored her spunk.

"What's that grin for?"

"Because, Dominic. Rachel is tending the bar and she just told some joker to fuck off when he asked her to strip. No way does she work the stage. Not from what she just said."

"Yet Rocco spoke as though he knew at least one of the strippers intimately..."

Xander frowned as he mulled over Jake's words, and his heart ached for Rachel.

"What's the bet that fucker is cheating on her."

"I imagine it would be almost unusual for a strip club owner to not sample his staff."

Joel's quiet comment was followed by Xander's growl. He couldn't hold it back.

"Bastard doesn't deserve her."

Jake sitting up straight had Xander's full focus instantly.

"And that, boys, is our cue to leave. You good to go Xander?"

Xander followed Jake's gaze to a group of men who'd just entered. Three of the men were from the farmhouse.

"Yeah, for tonight. Let's get out of here."

Chapter One

Seven weeks later.

With a small gasp, Rachel paused after she wrapped her fingers around a cold beer glass. A tingle had just run up her spine and her stomach filled with butterflies, which could only mean one thing. *He* was back. Every time he stepped through Classic Convicts' door Rachel was instantly aware. For almost two months he'd come in nearly every night. For the most part he simply watched her, staying silent. Sometimes he'd have a friend or two with him, but even then, he rarely spoke—which was such a pity, in Rachel's opinion. His voice was deep and commanding, with just the right touch of roughness to it. She could listen to him talk all night. She took a deep breath and shook her head, trying to settle herself.

The sad thing was, he'd never spoken more than a quick greeting and drink order to her. She'd never worked up the courage to ask anything more personal so she still didn't even know his name. But she always knew when he was near, and not just because of his appearance. Against her will, her mouth watered every time she saw that incredibly tall, muscular body of his that commanded attention. *Especially mine.*

Without turning from where she faced the back wall she knew, not only was he here, but he was focused on her. His gaze was hot and intense and it affected her in ways it shouldn't. Her body buzzed with anticipation, heat pooled between her thighs and her mind went a little fuzzy. Rachel shook her head to clear it. *I am an engaged woman, dammit!* As she turned with the glass in her right hand, she ran her left thumb over the band of gold on her third finger to remind herself. Rocco owned her, she wasn't free to lead on sexy men, no matter how much she wished otherwise. She had two choices, go back to England whcrc hcr parents wanted her to be a hermit, never leaving the house except for work, or stay here with Rocco.

"That big bastard back again?"

Speak of the devil... Rachel tried to contain her sigh. Rocco could be such a possessive idiot. At least, in some ways he was. He'd never handled her looking at other men well, but before this new bloke, he'd laughed at the attention she attracted from male customers both here in Classic Convicts, and down in HoHaven. Sold more drinks, he'd told her. He used the same excuse when he groped her behind the bar. She detested when he did that and she'd told him more than once to cut it out. It made her feel like a blow-up doll, here only for his pleasure whenever he wanted it. The sleazy old men who sat at the bar each night loved every second of it and always attempted to convince Rocco to put her around a pole on stage. Rocco always refused, and Rachel wondered why. She had good rhythm and used to love dancing the night away at nightclubs in London. Rocco had to know that with the amount of time she'd been behind the bar watching the girls do their thing around the poles, she'd worked out how to do a move or two. Hell, she'd even snuck down after hours a few times to try some of them out. She'd had a ball, cranking the music up and strutting her stuff to an imaginary crowd. She chewed her lower lip a moment. As much fun as she'd had, Rachel wasn't sure about having a real crowd watching her, or having strange men shoving money at her, trying to tuck it into her knickers. Yeah, that side of it still scared the shit out of her.

"I want you to go get ready for HoHaven to open."

With a frown Rachel shook free of her thoughts and glanced at her watch. It was an hour earlier than she normally left.

"Already? Have you got a party booked in or something?"

"No. Nothing special booked."

On a gasp her whole body tensed when he quickly wrapped his arm around her to take a bruising grip of her breast. He lowered his mouth to her ear where he roughly nipped her lobe.

"Don't argue, pet. Just do what you're told like a good girl."

Rachel held her breath to prevent a whimper leaving her. She wouldn't give him the satisfaction of crying out. Especially here with so many watching her.

"Rocco, you're hurting me."

Her hoarse whisper was quiet but she knew he heard

her. He released her with a chuckle and slapped her ass as he moved away from her to shake hands with the bastards at the bar watching her with lust in their eyes.

Blinking back tears, she turned and strode from the bar. Grateful she lived in the apartment upstairs, she didn't stop until she was in her bedroom. Normally she didn't bother coming up here to change, it was simpler to take her bag down to HoHaven and use the waitress' locker room. Generally, she was changed and out of there before any of the other staff came in. She was the owner's fiancé and as the bar manager, she was their boss which meant none of them were overly friendly with her. Out on the floor they were civil, but out in the real world, none of them wanted to know her. Like the dancers, a lot of the waitresses tried to throw themselves at Rocco. And wasn't jealousy a bitch? Rachel rubbed her tender breast. *If only they knew what they were jealous of, they wouldn't be.*

Working hard to keep his cool, Xander clenched his jaw. The bastard had hurt her. His mate was injured and he couldn't comfort her, or seek vengeance. Yet.

"You can't go over there, Xander."

He growled at Joel.

"I'm sorry, man. I really am. I wish we could just go over there and tear him to shreds like he deserves but we can't. Look around. Of the Triggers we've identified there's half a dozen of them here in the bar. We can't blow this by going in early."

Xander knew Joel was right. Didn't mean he had to like

it.

"When we get home I want to review everything we have so far. It's been a week since we've been able to all meet together and update on where everyone is at. We're going to have to make a move soon. Rocco's getting rougher with her. What he did tonight was because of me. He's noticed me watching her and doesn't like it."

"Well, of course the bastard doesn't like it. He treats her like shit and he's worried if she sees an easy way out from under his thumb she'll jump at it."

Xander turned to Sean, "What do you mean 'out from under his thumb'?"

"Like you said, it's been a week. I've been doing a little research on Miss Rachel Bell. I couldn't figure out why she stayed here. I mean, Rocco is an abusive prick and she just takes it. So I took a look into her current situation. Xander, she basically has no choice but to stay here if she wants to stay in the country."

Xander had wondered the same thing, why she stayed with him.

"What are you saying Sean? It's not like he keeps her under lock and key when she's not working."

Because like a stalker, he followed her when she did her weekly trip to the laundromat, so he knew she had at least some freedom.

Sean shook his head. "He's trapped her more securely than that. Rachel has one bank account, and it looks like Rocco has access to it on internet banking. I couldn't find any record of him having a card to it. But he has enough control over it that it never has more than a couple hundred bucks in it. Her mobile is blocked from international calls, both in and out. Dude, she's British. Having at least incoming international calls would be important to her, I imagine."

"And what's the bet he's not told her about it being an option. No doubt she believes that's simply how mobile phones work in Australia."

Joel leaned in as he added his opinion. "Or she doesn't know it's blocked and thinks her family back home doesn't care about her anymore. That would be my guess. There's no landline. Rachel has no way of calling her parents."

Xander's mind whirled with this news. He couldn't imagine not being able to contact his folks whenever he wanted. "What about email? Social media?"

"From what I've been able to hack into she doesn't write often. From her earlier emails, I get the feeling she never really felt at home in England and she loves living in Australia. She hasn't done anything with her social media stuff since coming to Tassie last April."

Xander frowned at Sean. By the pinched look on his face he had more dirt and he didn't want to say it.

"What aren't you telling me?"

"From what I've found, it's pretty clear Rocco's using the threat of getting her deported to keep her in line."

Rage heated his blood. "How in the hell is he doing that? This is 2013, not the 1920s!"

"She came to Australia on a Working Holiday Visa, most likely intending to backpack her way around the country for twelve months. Following the paper trail, she was fruit picking up the coast of Queensland when her year was up so she applied for a second visa. It was approved without an issue. Eight months ago she moved here with Rocco. I doubt she'll get a third Working Holiday Visa, and a Skilled Worker Visa, which would have her here on her own merits, won't fit with her bartending—it isn't exactly a special skill where the immigration department is concerned." Xander was about ready to shake him when he paused with a wince. "I did find a newer application filed with her name attached to it. For a Spousal Visa. I'm pretty sure that's why she's wearing Rocco's ring. She wants to stay in Australia and knows her options are limited."

Xander pressed his clenched fists into his thighs beneath the table. "I'm sure there's another way for her to stay here that doesn't include marrying that bastard."

Sean nodded. "I haven't taken the time to look at Immigration's skilled workers list, but there may be something she could do on there. But how the hell is she going to find out about it? I can't see Rocco telling her about her options, and we've all seen how coldly the other staff treat her here and next door."

"Look alert, we've got incoming."

Jordan's low voice had Xander glancing over toward the bar in time to see Rocco on his way to their table with a wicked looking frown marring his face.

"Just fucking great."

"Do not kill him. At least, not yet."

Xander rolled his eyes at Joel. "I'll do my best. You

boys do remember I'm meant to be in charge here right?"

They all grinned and spoke together. "Yes, boss."

"Smartasses."

He shook his head with a chuckle, grateful his friends had managed to lighten his mood a little before he had to face off against Rocco.

"Evening boys. Enjoying your night so far?"

"Can't complain. Can we help you?"

The bastard narrowed his gaze at Xander.

"Yeah, you can. By keeping your eyes off my woman."

Xander raised a single eyebrow at Rocco's threatening tone before he moved to stand. Rocco stood maybe six feet two, so when Xander rose to his full six feet six height, he dwarfed the man easily.

"Rachel is a gorgeous lady. There's nothing wrong with simply admiring beauty is there?"

His gaze tracked Rocco's Adam's apple bob as he swallowed. "No, guess not. Just wanted to make it clear she's not available."

"Well, while we're making things 'clear', if I ever see you lay a hand on her like you did tonight, you'll be paying for it. Do you understand? I'm not the kind of man to ignore violence against a woman."

Xander spoke in a low voice filled with malice. There was no way Rocco could misinterpret the underlying threat to his health. And going by the fear in the man's eyes, he'd received the message that Xander would not be intimidated by Rocco.

"I do believe it's time for you boys to leave for the

night."

The security guy who normally guarded HoHaven's door had appeared by his boss's side.

"No need to worry, mate. We were just having a little chat and clearing the air. Isn't that right, Rocco?" He clapped Rocco hard on the shoulder before turning back to his boys. "C'mon, let's get out of here. Time we should be heading home anyhow."

Resting his hands on his hips, Rocco winced as he watched the four men leave his bar.

"You want me to tail them, boss? Teach that big one a lesson for messing with your girl?"

Hmm, that could work. He needed to get some information on those boys. If they'd just come in a couple of times he wouldn't have worried, but they'd become regulars. And Rachel paid way too much attention to that bald one. Rocco couldn't give a flying fuck if men ogled his girl. Hell, it often boosted sales. But when she started looking back, then they had a problem.

"Tail them, but don't let them see you. I want to know where he sleeps and with who. I'm serious, Jimmy. No touching them. At least not yet."

"You got it boss."

With that Jimmy was out the door. Damn. Rocco hoped he didn't try to take on that group. By the look of them they worked out and knew how to handle themselves—Jimmy would end up losing that battle for sure. The bastard might be big, but he was dumb as a post and had no real skill with fighting. He was all scary window dressing.

Spinning to head behind the bar, he cursed to himself. If they hadn't lost so many men to the leopards last year, he'd have all the information he'd need by now. But no, the bastards had killed their tech guy and their man who'd managed to tap into the local police. Now all his research had to be done old school, which took forever.

The old boys at the bar all ribbed him about sending Rachel off early, but a free drink each and guarantees she'd be back working tomorrow night had them happy again. Without Rachel, his bar wouldn't be half as popular as it was. She was fucking beautiful, with lush curves, and that British accent was sexy as fuck. Men, old and young, were drawn to her and she knew how to work a crowd.

Between pulling beers, he rubbed the back of his neck. The Trigger higher-ups wanted his sole focus on tracking down shifters but he couldn't just neglect his woman and allow her to be snatched out from under him. A throbbing started up behind his left eye and he cursed again. Why'd he send her off so early for? Now he was stuck here till Roger showed up.

"Hey, boss. You okay?"

Speak of the devil.

"Only a headache, but I'd appreciate you taking over early so I can go get it taken care of."

The man knew him too well and smirked knowingly.

"Sure thing, boss. Go enjoy yourself."

With a nod, Rocco headed to the door that lead to HoHaven. Who was on tonight that would be here this early? Running through the names he pushed open the door and headed past the main area back to the hallway that ran past the change rooms and ended at his office. Poor sweet Rachel had no idea he rarely made it to his office without detouring into one of those rooms. He strolled into the working girls' room like he owned the joint, because, well, he did.

"Evening ladies. Ready to go?"

He glanced around at all his half-dressed girls. It was still a good half-hour before any of them would be out on stage so they were mostly naked and just starting to get ready. His dick stood straight up and throbbed at the sight of all these willing women coming toward him. He'd been inside each and every one of them. No self-respecting strip club owner didn't trial the merchandise before he put it on sale.

Candy reached him first and he slapped her ass as she pressed her big fake tits up against his chest with a purr. Her hand slipped low and she stroked him through his slacks.

"You're looking hungry, boss."

"Like you wouldn't believe. Looks like you get to start work early tonight, Candy. Get your ass down to my office."

She rolled her body against Rocco before she moved away to grab a satin dressing gown. He'd have preferred to watch her in nothing but a g-string as she prowled down the hallway, but back here in the halls it got fucking cold and he didn't need his girls getting sick on him.

That, and he couldn't risk Rachel catching him with a basically naked Candy. If she happened to catch him while she wore a robe, he could tell her he was doing a staff appraisal or something. He grinned. Yeah, he was totally about to appraise Candy, but good.

He followed her into his office, shut the door, flicked the lock, then went for his fly.

"Lose the robe, and on your knees. You know what I want."

Chapter Two

Jake took a sip of beer as he looked around the table. This was the first Anti-Trigger Team. He was rather proud of his eldest son, Dominic, for suggesting it. Generally speaking, snow leopard shifters were a peaceful race. They would fiercely protect their own when cornered, but never before had Jake heard of a team going after those who hunt them. While Trigger have been hunting their kind basically since they were first created, in the last decade they'd stepped up their attacks, getting more vicious and deadly with their assaults. Jake swallowed past the lump in his throat as he thought about his leap brother, Nick. Trigger had killed him and taken his body three months ago when the man had been working the rally near their home town.

Such a waste. Nick was so young, on the verge of adulthood. Now he was gone. His parents didn't even have a body to bury. The whole situation was torturous.

Pushing his grief down, Jake focused on taking another drink. He was alpha, but he hadn't been able to keep his leap safe from Trigger when they'd attacked. It had been his son, the future Alpha who'd stepped up and led the way. Dominic had taken a group of their best fighters to clean house. Of course, without Kit they'd not have known where to attack.

He looked across the table at her. Tall and lean with fiery red hair, she laughed as she ribbed her leap brothers. Kit was the fighting expert, trained by her father in martial arts from the time she could walk, and she had amazing skills. She was training the whole team to be better at defending themselves without having to shift or use weapons. Jessie, her mate and husband, sat by her side with an arm around her shoulders. He was slightly taller than Kit with short, light brown hair. Like Kit, he was South American and had the tanned skin tone to prove it. Jessie was a rally driver and knew cars inside and out. He was also pretty good in a fight, which made him a handy addition to their team. Jake could see using his rally schedule in the future to plan other trips to trace Triggers and Lost Ones alike. Searching for Lost Ones had been Jake's original plan for this team. Lost Ones were snow leopard shifters that had gotten separated from their leaps and lost in the world. Shifters like Kit, who'd been kicked out of homes, and ended up on the streets of Sydney before going bush to try to survive. Jake would never forget the sight of Kit as he'd first seen her—a mostly starved, scared out of her mind cub.

The door swung open and Xander, Joel, Jordan and Sean strode in, all frowning and throwing off a cloud of pissed off Jake didn't need his enhanced empath skills to detect.

"What happened?"

With a grunt Xander dropped into a chair. "Sorry we're so late. Rocco decided to warn me off *his girl* tonight and that apparently includes having one of his goons follow me home."

Jake stared at Xander's knuckles, then those of the other men, happy to see them all unscathed.

"What did you do to him?"

Xander shrugged. "Nothing. Just wandered around until we were sure we lost him."

Joel chuckled. "Yeah, he was a big bastard, but not too bright. I'm sure he had no idea we were onto him. He probably just figured we were taking the scenic route home."

"You did lose him, right? He doesn't know we're living here?"

"Calm down, Jake. We made sure we were free of him before coming back—and even if they do work out where we live, they have no idea who we are."

Jake frowned at Xander. It wasn't like him to not see the bigger picture.

"Seriously? You'd be happy for them to have our address? What happens once they do work out who we are? We're playing a game of cat and mouse here, and hoping we're sneaky enough to work out where all the mice are before one of them notices the big cat watching them all!"

Jake took a couple of deep breaths to calm himself down a notch as Xander lowered his gaze on a mumbled apology. He was glad he'd decided to take the time to oversee this first assignment for the team. Xander needed to get his head on straight. Jake understood that for Xander, with his mate on the line, this was a more intense situation than he'd have anywhere else. But in a way, the added stress on this first job was a good thing. It would show Xander exactly what was involved in leading the team and whether he thought he was up to the job full time. Jake was basically making the man an Alpha of his own small leap with this team. He hoped like hell he hadn't made a mistake giving Xander the role.

"Okay. Let's get this meeting started. Xander?"

The younger man straightened his shoulders and with a nod, took control.

"Right. We've managed to snap photos of around thirty associates of Rocco who may be Triggers. Sean? You and the twins have any luck getting names and addresses yet?"

"Joel and Jordan got me enough information to discount a number of them as not being involved with Trigger. We have several names of guys we think are, but we're still working on doing full profiles. We need to be positive they are Trigger before we go after them, so that's why we haven't passed on anything to the rest of you yet."

Jake sat back and observed as the meeting continued. He had a good feeling about where this project was going. Xander needed to be the leader of something, and this team was perfect. Jake also rather liked that he was going to be involved in the first offensive attack by shifters against Trigger. He couldn't wait to turn the tables on those bastards.

Rachel woke with a start as a loud snort filled the air. She opened her eyes to find Rocco sprawled out beside her fast asleep and snoring. *There goes any chance to sleep in for me.* With a sigh, she rolled over and slid from the mattress. She attempted to stand but had to sit back down when cramps wracked her lower belly. Pressing her palms against the pain, she silently cursed Rocco. He'd been rough with her after he'd crawled into bed earlier this morning. Taking a deep breath, she slowly rose to her feet and shuffled into the bathroom. Hopefully a steamy shower would help ease things.

As the hot water hit her body it soothed her muscles, and her nerves. He'd been in a foul mood all night—ever since he'd seen her admirer in Classic Convicts. She'd heard the waitresses gossiping about how Rocco had attempted to take the guy on but Jimmy had stepped in to smooth things over and toss the guy from the building. A grin tugged at her mouth. She would love to see her mystery man hand Rocco his ass in a fight. Rocco acted tough, and the man was built well. Years in gyms meant he had the muscles to back his mouth up. In theory. When it came down to it, Rocco didn't like getting his own hands dirty. Rachel was certain it had been years since Rocco had been in any physical altercations.

Once she'd scrubbed her body clean and washed her hair, she turned off the shower and stepped out from behind the curtain... and screamed.

"What the fuck, Rocco? You scared the shit out of me!"

Rubbing a hand over her pounding heart she grabbed

her towel with the other one and started drying herself. *Please don't let him be looking for another round.*

"I woke up to discover you'd snuck off on me, babe. I wanted to make sure you were okay."

She shrugged one shoulder. "I'm a little tender but I'll survive."

"Oh shit, I'm sorry, babe. I didn't mean to hurt you. I just... I don't know. I guess I needed to make sure you knew you were mine."

A snort escaped her throat, "You leave little doubt in anyone's mind that I belong to you, Rocco. You don't need to brand me."

One minute she was toweling dry her hair, the next she was pressed up against the wall with his hand wrapped in the wet strands and his body pressing hers face-first against the cold tile.

"Don't get smart with me, pet. Or I may just decide to brand you for real."

Fear had her heart pounding so loud she could barely hear Rocco's growled words. She pressed her palms against the wall and tried to push him back but he didn't budge. Instead the hand not in her hair came around to the wrap around the front of her throat. He squeezed firm enough that she went limp in his grip. She knew this game—until she stopped fighting against him, he wouldn't stop.

"Hmmm, that's better. You go all soft and docile when I wrap my fingers around your throat. Maybe I need to put a collar on you instead of branding you. Maybe then you'll be like this for me all of the time."

Bile rose up from her belly and tears stung her eyes. He lowered his mouth to her jawline where he proceeded to bite his way along the edge as he ground his fully-erect penis against her butt. She whimpered. She hated that the sound escaped but she couldn't hold it back. He growled in response.

"As much as I'd love to take you again, I don't have time. I have a meeting this morning... so it'll have to wait."

A moment later he released her and stepped into the shower himself. As she listened to the water pound against the tiles, she tried to get her breathing under control. Rocco's mood swings were getting worse. She stumbled out into the bedroom and leaned against the dressing table as she fought to calm down. She looked in the mirror and the grey smudge on her throat glared back at her. She raised her hand to finger the bruise. *Dammit, this can't keep happening.* She closed her eyes and took a deep breath. Thank fuck she healed fast. With a groan, she moved to open her closet and get dressed for her day. Not wanting to anger Rocco any more than he already was, she picked a pair of olive colored cargo pants and a loose fitting white button up shirt that she knew he would approve of. Heaven forbid she show any hint of her curves outside the bar or club.

She grabbed out her hairdryer and quickly dried her hair off, leaving it unstyled. She had the sides clipped short and normally styled the longer top section into a modern mohawk type thing. A silent FU to Rocco she'd started doing about six months ago after he went through her wardrobe and tossed everything he didn't 'like'. But this morning she didn't have the concentration needed to do it... nor did she have the time. She wanted to at least be on her way out by the time Rocco came out of the bathroom. Today was Monday, which meant it was laundry day. Rachel always took their washing down to the laundromat mid-morning to get it all done before she was due to start working in the bar late afternoon.

She'd just tied the bag of washing up when Rocco emerged from the bathroom.

"You're not going out like that are you?"

She frowned down at herself as her stomach tensed. What had she done wrong this time?

"What do you mean? I thought you liked this outfit."

He walked over to her and held her chin with his thumb and finger. "No makeup, babe. You can't go out without it on."

Fuck. She'd never been big on wearing makeup but Rocco insisted she always wear it, even if she was just going to the damn laundromat. Living with her parents' confining rules was starting to look not so bad.

"I was waiting for you to finish with the bathroom, Rocco. I wasn't going to go out without it on."

He frowned at her a moment before he roughly kissed her lips, bruising them until she whimpered.

"Good girl."

With that, he released her and she rushed into the bathroom before he could find some other fault with what she was wearing. Maybe later he'd be in a calmer mood and she could talk to him about him toning down his roughness with her. Leaving her bruised was not on, and it wasn't something he'd done before these past weeks. She frowned into the mirror as she coated her face with foundation. Could his decline in behavior be all related back to her checking out her mystery man? Was he really that jealous? She rolled her eyes—yeah, right. If Rocco was actually worried about her leaving him, he'd treat her better, not worse.

"Settle down, Xander. She's just running late."

Kit sighed into the phone as she watched Xander pace the footpath on the other side of the road from where she stood. Every Monday Rachel did her laundry here, and Kit had made sure she was here each week to chat with the woman. Generally speaking, Rachel kept a tight schedule and even though Kit wouldn't admit it to Xander, she was a little worried about her being so late too.

"And about time. She's heading your way."

"Well, you better vanish then. You're a little distinctive and she'll know who you are if she catches sight of you."

"Yeah, I know. I'll go back to my spot in the shadows. Damn woman is going to send me to an early grave with all the worrying she makes me do."

Kit winced at the pain in his voice. "It'll all work out, Xander. We'll get her free of that bastard and with you soon."

"I hope so. Okay, she's about to enter. Talk later."

Kit slipped her phone into the pocket of her jeans and turned to slap the button on the machine behind her to start it up. She'd set things up to look like she was partially through a load, so hopefully Rachel wouldn't clue in to the fact Kit was waiting for her. When the door made its usual squeak, Kit turned around to feign shock at seeing Rachel. But it turned out she didn't need to fake anything. With a growl Kit marched over to Rachel and pulled the collar of her shirt aside. Beneath a healthy layer of makeup were fresh bruises.

"Who hurt you, Rach?"

"Back off, Kit. I'm not in the mood."

Kit's phone chimed in her pocket with a message. She stepped back off Rachel to pull it free. She was fairly sure it would be Xander and she didn't want him barreling in here and blowing her cover with Rachel.

What happened?

Kit rubbed the bridge of her nose. Yep, Xander. He'd seen her confront Rachel. How to handle this so he doesn't lose his temper...

Not sure exactly. Give me some time with her.

She was putting her phone away when it chimed again. Cursing under her breath she pulled it back out.

Stay away from front windows. Rocco's man watching from parked car.

"Shit." Just what she needed.

Did he see me with Rachel?

No. Pulled up after.

Where?

Green ute.

Kit grabbed a five dollar note and headed for the change machine near the door. As she waited for her money to be converted to coins she casually glanced outside, spotting the ute half a block down. He wouldn't be able to see much from where he was, but was probably set to follow Rachel when she left. Kit returned to where Rachel was shoving clothes into a machine with more force than necessary.

"Sorry, Rach. I didn't mean to jump you as you came in. You're a little later than normal and I was getting concerned, then I saw your bruised throat. You're my friend and I'm worried about you."

Rachel stopped what she was doing and turned to face Kit with a shocked expression.

"You consider me a friend? All we ever do is wash our clothes together once a week."

Kit held her gaze. "And we chat. For a couple hours once a week we talk. That's more time than most friends spend together each week. Was it Rocco that left the bruises? What the hell did he do to you?"

With a shake of her head, Rachel rolled her lips in as her eyes moistened. She twisted to return to what she'd been doing when Kit couldn't hold herself back. Kit reached out and gently gripped her shoulder.

"I can help you, Rachel. If you want to get away from him."

Rachel's shoulders rose and fell before she faced Kit again, completely stone-faced.

"It's nothing, Kit. I bruise easily, but thankfully they

never last long. This will be completely gone by nightfall. Don't worry yourself over it, okay?"

Realizing she wasn't going to get Rachel to admit to anything, Kit let her hand fall away from her shoulder.

"Okay, I'll leave you alone for now. But promise me that if you ever do need help, you'll ring me. You can trust me, Rachel."

"Sure, Kit. I'll call you... if you give me your number."

Kit chuckled as she took Rachel's phone from her. "Well, yeah. A phone number would certainly help things along wouldn't it?"

She tapped her details in and saved it to her phone book, then sent herself a message so she had Rachel's.

"Right, and I have yours. Now we can ring during the week and chat whenever the mood strikes us. Maybe even go out for a coffee or something. Jessie calls us the laundry ladies. He thinks I don't know, but I heard him talking to the others."

Rachel frowned like she was trying to remember something. "Jessie isn't a firie like you is he?"

"Nope. My man's a rally driver. He's between races at the moment so he decided to come hang out with us firies that came on exchange."

"Yeah, not sure I understand the whole exchange thing either. What, like exchange students? But to the next town?" She shook her head.

Kit got her confusion.

"Like I said before, it's a team-building thing. Our station at Rosebery has a reputation for having really strong teams that function well out in the field. This exchange is the first of many as we move around and help other stations build up their teams to function like well-oiled machines."

"Uh huh. Hobart is so close to Rosebery, why don't you just run classes and go back home afterward?"

Kit chuckled. "Rosebery is about a four hour drive, so hardly a trip I want to do twice a day, every day." She shrugged. "And this is kind of a trial run. If it runs well, we'll head over to the mainland to help interstate firies. If it fails, we can simply run along home."

"And you're the only girl? And you're planning on moving around the country with a bunch of men." Rachel shook her head again. "Not sure I could do it."

Kit laughed. "Sure you could. Xander, Sean, Joel and Jordan are like brothers. I've known them since I was a teenager. And I always have Jessie with me. Why wouldn't I want a job that means I get to follow my husband around when normally I'd be left missing him for weeks at a time while he races?"

"I don't know much about rallying but I figured most of it was international, not interstate."

Kit grinned. "Yeah, I'll be taking leave for those races. We're still newlyweds, so I can get away with it for now."

A beep had Kit moving the wet clothes from the washer to the dryer and sliding in a few coins to set the thing going. This paying for each load had knobs on it. There was a perfectly functioning washer and dryer back at the house. Xander better appreciate what she was doing for him. Her phone dinged with a message just as she noticed the green ute move to a parking space in front of the window. Just great. She glanced at her phone to confirm it was only Xander telling her about the moving ute. Yep. Xander.

"Are you shitting me?"

Turning to face Rachel, Kit cocked an eyebrow. "What's up? Your machine playing up?"

"Nah, just Rocco being a dick again. Like I need supervision to wash clothes? Gah! Men."

Making sure she faced away from the windows, in the unlikely event the idiot in the ute could lip read, Kit caught Rachel's attention.

"Just say the word, Rach. My team and I will get you out of there and away safe."

The bittersweet smile Rachel flashed at Kit just about broke her heart.

"Life is never that simple, Kit. I can't just up and go." She sighed as she turned back to her machine. "I don't want to let him know we're friends. He can be possessive."

"I understand."

Kit went back to fussing around with her washing as she mentally went through options of how she could get Rachel away from Rocco. Maybe Jenny would have some ideas. Dr Jenny Reid was a shifter and a shrink, she might know of some loophole in the immigration system for abuse cases. It was definitely a lead worth checking out anyhow.

Chapter Three

Flipping through the pages Sean had handed him, Xander was impressed. Between the twins' computer skills and Sean's ability to see patterns in information and how he seemed to just 'know' how to put shit together to reveal any secrets that might be hidden beneath, he now had full profiles on eighteen Triggers linked to Rocco in front of him. Home and work addresses, who had wives and kids… hell, he was kind of surprised they hadn't listed the brand of toilet paper each of them used.

"You boys did an awesome job with this. How many more have you got to do before you're finished?"

Joel leaned forward in his seat. "Another six we still need to go through. I don't want to make any mistakes and take out someone not involved."

Xander nodded. "I agree, and we won't be touching any of the wives or kids. They're not a threat to us. If any of the wives know what their husbands are up to, the fact they all vanish will hopefully be enough for them to leave us the hell alone. However, we should keep an eye on them for a while after we raid. Just to be sure they're not planning any kind of retaliation."

Sean rubbed the back of his neck. "My instincts say Trigger doesn't care for women at all. They tolerate their men having wives, but no way would they permit one in their operation. I don't believe we'll have an issue with any families left behind, but keeping an eye on them for a while couldn't hurt."

Xander nodded before moving on. "Right, that's sorted for now. When we attack, taking out Classic Convicts will be our first strike. If we can line it up with a meeting, we can catch a good number of these bastards in one place. From what you've found out, it looks like they meet at least once, but sometimes two or three times a week. It shouldn't be hard to line it up. Sean? I need you to find floor plans for me. We've only seen the public rooms, and we need to know where all the exits are and any other space someone might use to escape us when we attack. We also need to use it to work out a plan to get Rachel out before we storm the place."

"I'll start looking first thing in the morning. It shouldn't be too hard to find."

Xander's pulse raced with how close they were to being ready. Like all shifters, he'd been brought up to fear and hate Triggers, but after having to watch Rachel suffer under Rocco for months, he had a whole new level of hatred for that bastard and was looking forward to taking him out.

Zipping and buttoning up his pants, Rocco slapped Cherry on the ass before he stepped back. His dick twitched when, with a sleek roll of her curvy body, the stripper straightened from where he'd bent her over his desk to fuck her from behind. His girls knew if they wanted something, they needed to pay a price.

"So boss, can I have the center pole tonight?"

With her shirt open and her bra pushed down, her tits were still pushed out and pointing at him. With his thumbs and forefingers, he gripped the rings through each of her nipples and pulled her toward him, her gasp and shudder kindling his erection back to full life. Before he could do anything about it, a sharp knock on the door had him releasing his grip with a curse.

"You'll use '*Doin' It*', and I want these on display. I'll be watching, and when you're done, you come to me. Understand? You want the center pole, you gotta work for it. Both before and after."

Cherry grinned up at him as she rearranged her clothing. "Like a please and thank you, huh, boss?"

"Exactly."

Watching her grind on the pole as the lights glinted off the little stones on her nipple rings as she shook those fake tits of hers would have him hard as a rock by the time she was through. Seemed logical she should take care of the situation she created. He'd just have to make sure Rachel wasn't around to see it.

Doing his pants up, he followed Cherry over to the door and opened it to let her out and his fellow Trigger in. He nodded at Mick. "You mind if we take this out on the floor?"

Mick smirked at him. "What? The preshow entertainment wasn't enough for you? This place reeks of sex."

Crossing his arms over his chest, Rocco didn't bother to answer with words. He simply grinned with a shrug of his shoulders. Owning a strip club had its benefits.

Ten minutes later, he sat at a rear booth where he had clear line of sight on the center pole. Mick was beside him and they both had a drink before them.

"Right, we've got about five minutes before I want to be focused on something else. What have you got for me?"

"You know that you're not seventeen anymore, right? Trigger doesn't run to the tune of your dick. You might be top boss here in Hobart, but if the higher ups learn of your little obsession with screwing anything in a skirt? You'll have big problems, mate."

Of course Rocco knew that.

"I pay attention when it counts. At the moment we're just doing recon. That can pause a few minutes to allow me some relief. Trigger doesn't expect me to close my business down for them."

Mick rolled his eyes but didn't comment further on his sex life. Fucker was just jealous.

"So, have you actually got some information for me or did you come here to talk smack about how I spend my free time?"

"Of course I have information. I wouldn't have come down here if I didn't."

"Well, spit it out!"

He opened his case and pulled free several sheets of paper. "I've been interviewing all the Triggers that were anywhere near Rosebery when that shit went down a couple months back. The shifters cleaned house pretty good but there were a handful not at the house when they attacked. They gave me descriptions of some of the shifters and I've been working on getting names. So far, I've only got a few. But I'm still working on it and have some leads I'm waiting to hear back on."

"Any of these names men we know?"

"I haven't personally heard of any of them, but I sure as shit am not gonna start hanging around Rosebery for the bastards to kill me!"

"Give me the list."

He held his hand out and Mick handed over the top sheet of paper. The list was short, only half a dozen, and some of the names were weird enough they'd stand out if he happened across them.

"What kind of fucked up names are Xander and Kit? Some douchey parents really called their kids that?"

"Doesn't that actor Vin Diesel play a dude called Xander in one of his films?"

Rocco shrugged. Like he gave a shit.

"Oh, and Kit is the only female on that list. From what I've discovered so far, it looks like all of them are firefighters out there. But I need to do a little more hunting before we go planning on blowing up the station or some shit. The higher ups have put their foot down on collateral damage of humans. Bastards."

He could say that again. So much easier if they could just go in and wipe out everyone there. Rocco didn't care if they were shifter or humans who hung out with shifters.

"You got any images to go with these names?"

"Not yet. I'm working on it. I'm waiting to hear back from a contact who was going to get me license photos. I should have them any day. Until then, here's some written descriptions that I got from my interviews."

At that precise moment, the lights dimmed and the music started. The first notes of '*Doin' It*' filled the room and with a grin, Rocco adjusted himself in the seat. He'd examine the descriptions later.

"Too dark out here now to read that shit. I'll look it all over later. You staying or going? You know you're welcome to hang here. If you want something off menu, just say the word and I'll make sure you're taken care of."

Mick just shook his head on a laugh. "I got a girl, don't need any others. I'll let you know when I hear anything more."

After a quick fist bump, Rocco was alone in the booth with his drink, and nothing to do but watch Cherry shake her ass and tits between grinding against the pole. *Fuck.* He adjusted himself once more. He couldn't wait for her to be grinding against *his* pole.

"Boss, bad news. Bella is off sick."

"Fuck me."

He scrubbed his face in both his hands. She was due up on center pole after Cherry finished. Who else could he put up there to keep the regulars happy? Bella Diamond was his main draw card. Especially on a busy Friday night. Half the men currently in the club were here solely to see her strip. He ran through who else was on tonight but none of them had Bella's skills or assets. He glanced around at the growing crowd as he pondered his options. He tensed when that big bald bloke came strolling in with his buddies. Fucking brilliant, just what he needed. He was another thorn in his side. Jimmy had lost them a fortnight ago and again last week, both times before he got any information on them. Well, other than the fact they know the back streets really well and can tell when they're being followed by a big dumb idiot.

Suddenly the solution came to him. He'd deal with two issues with one stone. He got asked daily to put Rachel around a pole, and Rocco knew she often came down here during the day to play around on the poles. And wouldn't it be fun to see that bastard's face when he realized the girl he's been drooling over is up on the stage showing her goods to every man in the joint?

Actually, Rachel was built along the lines of Bella, so maybe with a wig and makeup, the regulars wouldn't notice. With the low light and a few drinks under their belts... it might work. It was worth a shot. He stood and made his way over to behind the bar.

Rachel blew out a shuddering breath as she climbed the stairs at the rear of the stage. What the hell was she doing? Sure she mucked around after hours on the poles but the main center stage? In Bella Diamond's place? Rocco must be fucking insane to think she could pull this off!

"Go on, get out there and do your thing. You'll hold everyone up if you take much longer."

With her heart beating louder than a drum, she forced herself to move forward. The first deep beats of '*Closer*' by Nine Inch nails pounded through the room, vibrating her body and relaxing her a little. Pretending like she strutted around in mile high stilettos all the time, she headed to the pole, imagining the room was empty like it was after hours and she was just here having a little fun and blowing off steam. She wrapped her fingers around the cold metal and did a slow body roll against it, sliding down to a crouch, allowing the strong beat of the song to flow through her, to dictate her movements. She rose up and as the first "help me" played she reached high to take hold of the pole and lift herself up. She did a slow spin before she inverted herself. Her lips spread into a grin as she held her weight off the ground with only the strength of her legs. Keeping one leg securely wrapped around the upper part of the pole, she spun a few times while moving her other leg out then back in.

With a quick twist she lowered herself to the floor. Releasing the pole she slid face first forward, keeping her ass in the air for a moment before she flattened out. Nerves had her hesitating as the cheers kicked up around her. She needed to start taking off clothing. Oh, fuck. She was going to be spank bank fodder. Bile rose but she forced it down. She could do this. Now she'd started, she couldn't back out. She didn't even want to contemplate what Rocco would do to her if she embarrassed him like that! His moods were getting more and more volatile since they moved to Hobart last April.

Moving over onto her back, she arched up before rolling onto her knees. A quick tug and her shirt was undone, revealing her tiny sparkling bra. She flatly refused to go fully naked on her first dance. Rocco seemed to understand that was a hard line for her so she'd be left wearing a tiny g-string and this minuscule bra when she was done. But it was better than going the full monty.

Rolling her shoulders, she allowed the filmy material to fall off to the floor before she did a body roll and stood. She strode back the pole and ground against it a little before she gripped it and did another spin or two, making sure she spread her legs to flash beneath her tiny skirt. The moment she landed, she flipped the clasp at the side of the skirt, and it too floated to the floor. She was now as bare as she was going to get and could get back to enjoying her routine.

She truly loved the rush of pole dancing. Relying completely on her own strength and skills, she spun once, then gripped the pole with both hands to hold herself sideways. Spreading her legs into a split, she grinned at a couple wolf-whistles that filled the air. Another spin and she twisted so she faced out with her legs around the pole beneath her. Her upper body was arched so her boobs were thrust out on full display. The cheers got even louder as she spun once more and body rolled to the music. Yeah, she was kind of getting into this. She could see why the girls did it. At least this part. The crawling around bit where the men all pawed her to tuck notes in her g-string and bra was the part she could do without, but her song was coming to an end and she needed to at least try to get some tips. She was fairly sure they knew she wasn't Bella, even with the blond wig and long fake lashes.

For her final move she spun up high before spiraling her way to the bottom, where she landed on her knees with them spread wide. Still holding the pole above her head, she rolled her body in time with the beat before she fell forward and with a slide crawl, made her way to the edge of the stage where way more men than she anticipated stood with notes in their hands. Shit. There had to be over a dozen. Could she stomach that many putting their paws on her? And where was Rocco? He didn't like her mystery man even staring at her, but he was fine with this?

Rachel's thoughts continued to whirl in a tailspin as she moved forward without missing a beat. She had her fake all-is-well mask firmly in place and was going to see this thing through. She barely withheld the shiver of disgust as the first man grabbed her ass before he slid money behind the string over her hip. She looked through the throng of men, trying to find something to focus on to get her through this part without puking on them all.

What caught her eye froze her in place. She only vaguely felt the hands on her now. Across the room, at a rear table, Rocco sat with Cherry on his lap, her nipple piercing between his teeth and his hands on her hips, holding her as he thrust up against her. Tears pricked her eyes. That wanker was cheating on her, and had the gall to do it right in front of her!

"What the fuck?"

Forgetting all about her routine she rose sharply, ignoring the men whining they didn't get a chance to paw at her. Her gaze was locked on her fiancé as he fucked another woman. A growl filled the room, louder than the music and she automatically sought out the source. Her mystery man had stood from another table and was focused solely on her. Fuck. He did not look happy. Guess he knew she wasn't Bella now, too. Shame filled her. Would he think less of her now? She blinked back tears as she turned and wobbled on her heels. She flicked them off, snatching them and her clothes as she ran from the stage. She flew down the steps and bolted for the back door. She needed to get upstairs. There she could lock herself in and ... Rocco had a key. Fuck. She couldn't go upstairs.

At a dead run, she shouldered her way through the change room door and, sending up a thank you that the room was empty, she unlocked her locker in record time. Where could she go? Kit. Would Kit let her stay over? Fuck. She didn't know her well enough to call her for something like this. She could end up in deeper trouble by running off with a woman she'd only met a dozen or so times at a laundromat. She had to confront Rocco while it was fresh. Before he had time to work out a way to convince her she didn't see what she had. She hastily wiped at the tears on her face and got tangled up in the stupid fake lashes. She peeled them off and tossed them onto a dresser, along with the tacky blond wig. She grabbed a wet wipe and roughly scrubbed her face. What a fucking mess...

A loud thump outside the door had her jumping and throwing her shirt and pants on over her stripper shit, including the notes that were poking her uncomfortably. She shut her locker and slung her bag over her shoulder. She'd get upstairs and shower then deal with Rocco when he came up later.

She was about to grab the door when it flung wide, nearly catching her in its wake.

"Whoa, bloody hell."

She could not catch a break tonight! Her mystery man stood before her in all his masculine glory. He was more than she could take, especially now while she was feeling so fragile. What would her life be like if she'd meet a man like him before she'd met Rocco? More tears left her eyes and wet her cheeks. It didn't matter, did it? Her life was, what it was and it didn't have a prince charming. Nope, just an asshole who screwed his working girls. All the rumors she'd discounted spun in her mind. How many had he fucked? All of them? Hell, he had like a dozen girls working the poles. She squeezed her eyes shut against the pain that tore her chest wide open.

Gentle fingers on her cheek had her rearing back with a yelp. She'd forgotten she wasn't alone.

"Don't. Don't touch me."

Tingles continued to tease the skin he'd touched and she lifted her palm to cover the flesh. What the hell was that about?

Fury and rage like Xander had never experienced before filled his body when he'd heard her precious voice curse from the stage. He'd been staring daggers at her asshole fiancé as he fucked one of his strippers in the middle of his fucking club, when he'd heard her sweet accent. He'd tried to go to her but Joel was with him and he'd gotten in his way and talked him down. The place had been crawling with Triggers and they couldn't show their hand yet. They were so close to being able to clean house here in Hobart, they couldn't blow it now. He knew his friend was right, but it burned to see his mate nearly naked and getting pawed at. If that wasn't bad enough, the agony etched on her face now as she stared at Rocco across the way nearly gutted him.

When she'd spun and ran off the stage, Rocco had glanced over, rolled his eyes and went on with screwing the girl on his lap. *Piece of shit bastard.*

He pushed Joel aside. "I'll be careful. But I have to go to my mate."

Keeping out of plain view, he snuck around the outside of the room to go backstage. By the time he got to the hallway, all the stages were full and no one guarded the entrance. *Guess all girls are out working now so there's no need.* Joel followed him as he thumped open the door to find himself in a long hallway. The door banged loud against the wall, but he didn't care. He'd kill anyone who came at him, or his mate. His mood was vicious and he'd like nothing better than to rip someone apart. Preferably

Rocco. Honing his hearing, he followed the sound of her sobs. His heart ached for her. She'd clearly had no idea about her fiancé's infidelities.

He thrust open the door closest to where he could hear her, and cursed under his breath. He'd nearly knocked her silly with the thing. As he stood there waiting for her to react to his presence, she stayed silent. Aside from that initial shocked cussing she now simply stood staring blankly into space as tears rolled down her cheeks. What was he meant to do with her? He wanted to pick her up and take her home, but he doubted that would end well. She'd never stay, and would hate him for taking her without consent.

"Baby girl?"

He stroked his fingertips down her wet cheek, loving the sparks of awareness that shot up his arm even though he ached that she was so upset. With a jerk, her eyes cleared and she recoiled from him, as though he were a snake.

"Don't. Don't touch me."

She palmed her cheek a moment before she dropped her hand and straightened her shoulders.

"Who the bloody hell are you? Have you any idea the shit you've caused for me?"

With a shake of his head he swallowed. "It wasn't me cheating on you tonight, baby. Don't transfer your anger to me. All I want to do is take care of you. I'd never treat you like Rocco does. Not ever." His gaze dropped to a fresh bruise just under her collarbone and a growl left him. "I'd certainly never mar your flesh with bruises. He doesn't deserve you."

She backed away, wide eyed and looking a little frightened.

"And you do? A man who stalks a taken woman for months?"

"Not stalking. I've been waiting for you to leave that fuckwit before I moved in and swept you off your feet."

She laughed at that, but it wasn't a happy sound. It was hollow and heartbreaking.

"I don't even know your name and you want to date me?"

He gave her a sad smile, "That's because getting anywhere close to you has been near impossible. Trust me, I would have introduced myself a lot earlier if I could have. I'm Xander Moore."

Xander frowned in confusion as she gasped and stepped further away from him, covering her mouth with her fingers as she shook her head. What did he say wrong?

"You're Kit's Xander? Oh, shit."

"Kit is like my sister, yes. Why is that an issue? I don't understand why knowing that would scare you."

"You don't? How stupid do you think I am? I've been using that laundromat for nine months and the week after you stroll into the pub that first time, she turns up there. Like clockwork, every week at the same time as me. I can't believe I didn't work it out sooner. But then, I didn't work out Rocco either so I guess I'm just that dumb. Who the hell are you and what do you want with me?"

Her gaze bounced around the room, no doubt looking

for either a weapon or an exit. He raised his palms up.

"I will never hurt you, Rachel. I want to protect you. Kit initially went to meet you because you're mine, but I think you'll find she's now claimed you as hers and will go to the ends of the Earth to protect you too."

"Sorry, I'm yours? No way. You cannot come in here and lay this on me! Especially not tonight. Not when I need to deal with—"

A sob cut her off and Xander couldn't stand it. He had to do something to comfort her. She was his mate and she was in pain. With quick steps, he reached her in seconds and wrapped her in a hug before she knew what was happening. He fought the urge to groan. She fit against him perfectly, proving how they were made for each other. He pressed a kiss to the top of her head, wishing it was her lips.

She nuzzled against him for a few moments before she took a shuddering breath and backed away. He wanted to hold her to him, but knew it was too soon for that. She was human. She didn't understand anything about the draw between them, and now was not the time to attempt to explain it. He could tell by the look in her eyes she was gearing up to say something to get rid of him. Her night had been shitty, and he could totally understand her wanting it over with.

Spying a pad of Post-It notes, he snatched it up along with a pen. He scrawled his mobile number down before handing the pad to Rachel.

"I'm going now, but if you need anything, anything at all, you call me. I'll answer no matter what time of day or night. The only time I won't answer will be if I'm at a fire, and if that's the case, you have Kit's number. You call her and she'll get to me."

She frowned as she took the paper from him.

"I don't get why you're doing this."

He caressed her cheek one last time. "You will, baby girl. One day I'll explain it all, but not tonight. You need to go have a bath, relax and get some sleep. If you can, lock that bastard out. He doesn't deserve you, and you shouldn't have to deal with his shit."

She opened her mouth and he knew he'd overstepped. Before she could say a word, he spun and left her standing there, holding his phone number, looking heartbreakingly fragile with her tear-stained face and rumpled clothes. But he couldn't hold her like he wanted. At least he couldn't yet. One day he would have that right, and that day would come soon. He'd make sure of it.

Chapter Four

Rachel was barely aware of her movements as she fled up the back stairs to her apartment. Her mind was whirling with thoughts of her mystery man. No, she knew his name now. Xander. Her mystery man was Xander Moore. His last name was appropriate, because damn, she wanted more, that's sure. She shook her head as she headed straight to the bathroom. Did she never learn? She needed to focus on dealing with Rocco's shit. She didn't need to add another man into the chaos that was her life. With a deep sigh, she decided she wouldn't be ringing those precious ten digits he'd given her. Nope. No way.

She peeled off the shirt she'd tossed on downstairs and winced as the notes stuck in her bra crinkled and poked at her. Damn plastic money. The corners hurt. Although, she guessed, knowing her luck, if there were paper ones, she'd have given herself paper cuts. She pulled the cash free and tossed it in a pile on the counter before she striped off the pants and repeated the process of gathering her tips. The pile she ended up with shocked her. How did those men have so much money to toss away like that? No way could she justify literally throwing her money away. Fingering through the various notes she spotted a reddish one.

Twenty dollars? One of them liked her performance so much he thought she was worth twenty dollars? Shaking her head at the insanity of it all she flipped the tap and stepped under the spray.

She scrubbed her body with relish, wanting nothing more than to rid herself of all the sweat—both hers and the other men. But when she got to her face she hesitated. She lightly ran her fingertips over her cheek where Xander had caressed her. She could still feel the memory of the sparks that had flared at his touch.

Calling herself a fool, she scrubbed her face clean too. When she closed her eyes to rinse her face under the spray, images of Rocco and that chick filled her vision. A groan echoed around the room as she turned the water off and stepped out to dry herself. Not wasting time, she was dry and in a pair of yoga pants and a baggy t-shirt within minutes. She paced the apartment. What should she do? Maybe she shouldn't have run away. If she were only braver, stronger, she would have gone over to him to call him on his cheating. Too late for that now. She could go back down there. Would he still be with her? She doubted it. He didn't have much stamina.

The door banged open and on reflex she jerked away from the sound.

"What the hell do you think you're doing, running off like that?"

Fury at what he'd done trampled her fear of him into the ground.

"Me? What the hell was I doing? What were *you* doing?

Screwing a dancer right in front of me? How the fuck did you think I'd react?"

Pain flared as his hand struck Rachel's cheek and she mentally kicked herself. She should know better than to yell at him. He'd never tolerated her raising her voice at him and in the last few months it always ended with her in pain when she forgot. Firming her jaw against the heat flaring in her cheek she glared at him.

"You don't swear at me, woman. Not ever. And you let your imagination run away on you. I was merely getting a lap dance. Nothing more. The girl needed to practice before she's ready to do it for paid clients."

"I saw her nipple piercing between your teeth, Rocco. I saw you holding her hips as you thrust up into her."

She kept her voice low and steady, being careful not to lose her temper and start swearing again.

"I gave her nipple ring a tug, so what? Part of a lap dance is grinding on the man's lap. That was all you saw."

He stepped up to her forcing her to retreat across the room, toward the bedroom.

"Let's go to bed and I'll make it up to you, even though I did nothing wrong."

Rachel was mentally rehashing what she saw. She was certain she wasn't mistaken. But maybe she had misread the scene she'd witnessed? Either way, she was not having sex with him tonight.

"I'm not the mood, Rocco. It's been a long day and an even longer night. I just want to sleep."

Her breath caught when his expression turned vicious

and his fists clenched by his sides. Oh, shit. This was going to be worse than his previous bouts of fury at her, she was certain.

"Not in the mood? You get all jealous when you think I had someone else, yet you won't put out?"

He grabbed a fistful of her hair and threw her against the wall. Her hands slapped the hard surface first but he'd thrown her with such force her forehead still cracked against the plaster. Pain filled her rattled mind as she was tugged away from the wall and spun around. Rocco's mouth was on hers, his teeth biting into her lower lip until she tasted the coppery tang of her own blood. She whimpered, but as usual he didn't care he hurt her. In fact, he seemed to relish it these days. How far was he going to go? Was tonight going to be the final time? When he pushed her too hard and killed her. She couldn't believe how much he'd changed since they'd moved to Hobart. He hadn't been violent in the least when they lived up on the Gold Coast last year.

As he began landing blow after blow she crumpled to the floor and covered her head with her arms and he switched from punches to kicks. An image of Xander filled her mind, his tough face etched with lines of concern and care, his touch gentle and kind. What would it be like to have that sort of male in her life? One that stayed nice. Tears sprung forth and she did nothing to stop the flow. She'd never get the chance, she was sure Rocco would make certain of it.

Washing the blood from his knuckles Rocco winced. He'd been too hard on her. He'd lost his damn mind when she'd turned him down. How dare his woman say no?

After drying off, he crept to stand at the bedroom doorway. She'd crawled from the floor to the bed where she lay curled into a tight ball. He took a deep breath. He couldn't undo what he'd done and it was certainly a lesson she'd remember. Rocco was sure that would be the last time Rachel ever refused him. Hopefully he'd never have to teach her a lesson again on that score.

Deciding to leave her be for now, he left the apartment and headed downstairs to his office. He needed to go over the information Mick had left him. He could put it off until he had photos but his gut told him waiting would be a bad idea, and he could use the distraction. Between the pressure of running this place, plus all the Trigger shit, he felt like he was losing his damn mind most days. He never used to be as angry as he was now that's for sure.

Sitting at his desk, he pulled open the folder and began reading.

"Motherfucker!"

He re-read the first description. Six feet six, bald, tattooed upper arms, dark eyes. It had to be the same man. Xander was the one who'd been sniffing around his girl. He quickly read the other descriptions. Identical six foot three twins with short dark hair and blue eyes. Rocco squeezed his eyes shut. He didn't need to read more. He'd seen those twins with the bald bastard enough times. What did it all mean?

Needing more information, he pulled his phone out and dialed a number he really didn't want to. Disturbing the higher ups was rarely in your best interest, but Rocco figured because he'd seen several known shifters along with having a woman they were clearly interested in, he'd fair well with Trigger's upper management.

After only one ring the call was answered.

"Confirm your identity."

Rocco rattled off his id number.

"Excellent. What do you require, Rocco? It must be dire for you to disturb us with it."

Even though they couldn't see him, Rocco sat straighter and swallowed past the lump in his throat.

"Ah, it's just come to my attention that a man who's been following my fiancé for the past two months is one of the shifters from the Rosebery massacre. In fact, he and a number of his shifter buddies have been coming in nearly nightly to my bar."

"And you do not know why he would be doing such a thing? While impressed you have identified them, I am most disappointed you do not know the reason behind his interest in your woman."

He winced at the reprimand in the man's tone. "With all due respect, sir, while I put all my free time into locating shifters for Trigger, I need to keep my business running too. I haven't had time to study up on the shifters' social habits."

A low sigh came over the line and Rocco knew he was getting close to crossing a line he couldn't come back from.

"Unlike humans, shifters only ever take one true mate in a lifetime. We are yet to work out how they know who their mate is, but as you have now witnessed, the males know by sight. Your fiancé is this male's mate. As such, she is to be viewed as one of them. Not human, but shifter and in need of containment. You have permission to use her as bait to catch as many shifters as you can. But if you cannot use her to bait a trap, you will turn her over to our custody. How do you wish to proceed?"

Blinking in shock, Rocco fell back in his chair. Fuck. He was going to lose his girl either way. He rubbed his face. What to do, what to do...

"I'll use her first."

"Good choice. I trust you received our package this past week?"

He patted his pocket. "Yes, I received the Taser and as instructed I've been carrying it with me at all times."

"Excellent. We expect no more bullet or knife wounds in our captives. Call us when you have captured any full blood shifters and we will send a team for collection. Oh, and Rocco? Do not try to hide Rachel from us. We know all about your activities outside your relationship with her, so you cannot possibly claim to truly love the girl. She is now our property and we will not be deprived of obtaining a shifter mate."

The line went dead before he could utter a response. Not that he would have. The unsaid threat that he would end up being taken in if he didn't do as they wished was loud and clear and Rocco got the message. He was expendable to his bosses and no matter how this all played out, he'd lose Rachel.

He rubbed his chin as he tossed his phone on the desk. Did he love her? She was pretty and had great oral skills, but he couldn't honestly say he had any strong feelings for her. Sure, he didn't want to lose her, but he could live without her just fine. As the bastard on the phone had said, he had plenty of other girls to keep him satisfied. Surely, finding another bar manager shouldn't be too difficult.

That was all of course, assuming he and his club survived the coming battle. How the hell could he set a trap with her as bait?

Tilting his head, Xander stretched out his neck before he continued pacing. Something had happened to his mate. His heart ached with her pain. She'd suffered, was still suffering. Two hours had passed since he'd left her in that changing room and for the past half an hour he'd battled the urge to rush to her side. He glared over at Jake. The Alpha of his leap had stopped him, forced him to not run off into the night to go take her.

"Stop shooting daggers at me. I just saved your hide. What do you think would happen if you alone went storming into a Trigger stronghold? I will not risk your life like that."

Xander snarled but stayed silent. While he understood Jake's logic in theory, it didn't mean he had to like it.

That bastard fiancé of hers had beaten her. With the level of pain he could feel from her, he was certain of it. In his head he had it all planned out—how he would enter the upstairs apartment through the old fashioned external fire escape stairs. He'd slip into her room, rip the throat out of that asshole, then take his mate with him and keep her protected while he got her any medical attention she might need.

If only Jake would release his hold on him. If it were someone else being locked down, Xander would have been impressed. He'd been unaware the Alpha had that particular power. Clearly, it was one Jake used extremely rarely.

Focusing back on his hypothetical plan to rescue his mate, he wondered if she'd go with him? She'd seemed scared of him earlier. Was she scared of all men, thanks to Rocco? She seemed fine in the bar and club, but that was public and with strangers she didn't have to see again. Up close and one-on-one, she seemed a different woman. Fearful and nervous.

"What the fuck happened? It sounded urgent."

Kit stood in the doorway a slight flush to her face. She'd been down at the station working, so Xander figured Jake must have called her in.

"We need to fast forward our plan. Jake is refusing to let me go in tonight, so tomorrow night we'll be shutting down Classic Convicts and getting my mate the fuck out of there."

"You know I've got your back and I'm all for going in, but what happened to up the time frame?"

Xander rolled his shoulders as he did another lap of the

room.

"He put her on stage tonight. She got to watch him screw another girl from up there."

Kit shook her head. "Seriously? That man is such an asshole. Everything I learn about the bastard just makes me want to kill him all the more. My mornings at the laundromat with her are turning into lessons in restraint."

"Actually, I'm not sure how she'll react next time you see her. I went after her when she ran off stage and we spoke for a bit. Once she learned my name, she put two and two together and wasn't too happy about us knowing each other."

Kit didn't look concerned. "We knew she'd work it out at some point. I've certainly made no attempt to hide my connection to you or the firehouse. Don't worry about it. I'm sure it'll all work out in no time once we save her ass from that dickhead Rocco."

His every muscle tensed. How he wished he could barge in there tonight and snatch her, but deep down he knew Jake was right. They needed a plan. Taking a deep breath he pushed his emotions down, and those he could still feel from Rachel.

"Alright, everyone take a seat and let's get this meeting started." He gave his team a couple minutes to get comfortable, before he focused on Sean. "Have you finished putting together floor plans?"

"Sure have." Sean rose to spread paper over the table. "Had to go old school to find these buggers, but I finally got hold of a set yesterday. Now these are old, so the internal layout might be different. But they can't move load-bearing walls so we know these are still in place."

Xander stayed silent as he listened to Sean describe the layout until he got to the exits.

"So, there's only two main entry points plus three fire escapes?"

Jordan nodded. "The entrance at the rear of the basement may be blocked completely. Under code they need it clear for a fire escape, but there isn't much about that club that's up to any kind of code, so I doubt Rocco cares about the necessity of a fire escape."

Joel, who'd been tasked with working out the routines of Rocco and any other Triggers they could find, leaned forward as he spoke. "That door is where they take deliveries—it's in full working order."

Xander looked over the plans trying to think of how to best storm the place.

"Who have we got available?"

He hadn't forgotten that they were officially in town to work with the local firehouse.

Kit crossed her arms over her chest. "The twins and I are on call, but we're not required at the station, so if there's no fire we're all yours."

"Okay, so with Jake we have a sure four, maybe seven. Jake? How many do you think we can pull in from Rosebery?"

The older man sighed as he took a moment to think. "We can't pull everyone. Some need to stay in case Trigger attack while we're away. But Dominic should be able to pull a team together and be down here."

"Do you think we could have Adele on hand? If we have any shifter injuries it would be good to have them taken direct to Rosebery Hospital rather than Hobart's."

Adele was Dominic's mate and a trained nurse and paramedic. She'd know how to treat any shifters. Conversely, if Rachel was hurt and taken to Hobart, he wouldn't be able to get in and see her. In Rosebery, the head of the hospital, Dr Clint Maynard, knew about shifters and mates and would allow him access, despite his not being direct family.

"I'll call Clint in the morning and see what we can work out. I wouldn't count on it though. Hobart hospital is too big to do what we do out at Rosebery. If Rachel gets taken in, you may be refused access."

Xander sent Jake a thankful glance. "I'll appreciate anything you and Clint can pull together." He turned back to the plans. "Right, let's talk strategy..."

Despite the fact he could still feel Rachel's pain, it had lessened like maybe she'd gone to sleep. Which meant his cat had quit prowling within him to be set free to go rescue her, allowing him to focus on how he could actually plan to do just that.

One way or another, he would have his mate with him where she belonged by tomorrow night. He would accept nothing less.

Chapter Five

With a groan, Rachel managed to haul herself out of bed and into the shower. It was well past noon and she'd not seen any sign of Rocco since last night. She wasn't sure if she was relieved or pissed off. For certain she was grateful there had been no round two of his physical violence, but where had he slept? Or should she say, with whom had he slept?

Tears pricked her eyes as the hot water rushed over her skin. She'd been such a fool. Just because she was honest and would never cheat on or lie to her partner didn't mean everyone else was that way. Even if Rocco was super possessive of her, that clearly wasn't a sign that he loved her.

Had he ever loved her?

Rachel thought back over their time together. He'd occasionally said the words, but he'd never really shown her had he? Other than wanting to keep her for himself, he didn't take her out. Hell, he hadn't even bought her a washing machine so she didn't have to trek down to the laundromat every bloody week to wash their clothes. She'd been asking for one since they moved in. Although, since meeting Kit there, she actually looked forward to the weekly excursion now.

Her mind filled with the concerned face of Kit and she stilled. Should she call her and ask for her help to escape? Running a cloth over her face reminded her of another concerned face—Xander. Kit was friends with Xander, so Rachel didn't know if she could trust her. Would they save her from Rocco just to capture her themselves? She shook her head with a humorless laugh. Great. She'd gone from trusting everyone instinctively, to trusting no one. Kit had never shown her anything but care and friendship. And in the past she would have called her in a heartbeat for help...but now, she couldn't do it. Couldn't trust her own judgment on whether the woman meant her harm in the long run.

Flicking off the taps she stepped out and dried herself off, thankful the hot water had loosened her muscles and eased her aches enough she could move around almost pain free. Never did she think she'd be so grateful for her quick healing abilities.

Calling Kit wasn't the answer. No, she needed to do this herself. She was an adult and could get herself free from Rocco. What she needed to do was work out another way to get a Visa to stay in Australia. Tasmania had captured her firmly in its grasp and she had no desire to leave the lush green state. Although, she would move away from Hobart. No way did she want to accidentally run into Rocco on the streets.

With a loose plan in mind she quickly dried and styled her hair and covered the bruises on her face and neck with makeup. She needed to find an immigration lawyer to help her, then she needed to find a cheap hotel. Surely she could find somewhere that needed a cook, bartender or waitress to help out in exchange for a room and food.

Feeling lighter with plan to escape settled, she grabbed a quick bite to eat before she headed downstairs to leave.

"What the bloody hell?"

The door was dead-bolted and the key was gone. The key was never removed. With a frown she scanned the floor. Maybe it fell out? After five minutes of searching the entire area she had to admit it was truly gone. Swallowing down her nerves, she headed down to Rocco's office in the basement. Hopefully he was at least in the house and hadn't locked her in and left. And hopefully he'd settled down out of his mood. Rachel really didn't want to talk to his fists again.

With a deep breath for courage, she pushed open the door to his office. He was sitting behind the desk looking like a king ruling over his minions. He looked up at her with a raised eyebrow. The bastard didn't even show an ounce of remorse for hurting her last night. *Fuck being independent, I need to get out of here any way I can.*

"The key's missing out of the front door. I need to go out for a bit this morning."

He calmly put his pen down before he sat back in his chair.

"The key is missing because I took it. You'll find all the doors are locked, including the fire escapes. You have no need to leave the apartment today, so you won't."

Fury burned through her veins, knocking her common sense straight out of her. "What the bloody hell are you playing at? You've never laid into me like you did last night, now this morning you're acting all high and mighty and keeping me locked in?"

Rage transformed his face and with a curse, Rachel turned to run. She didn't get far before Rocco was on her. She groaned as he slammed her hard against the wall. Using her hair he pulled her face away from the plaster to growl in her ear.

"I'm not the one playing, Rachel. You are. A very dangerous game that you should've known you'd never win."

Pushing past the sting of him pulling her hair, she frowned in confusion.

"I'm not playing any game, Rocco. I just wanted to go to the shops this morning. Why can't I leave the house?"

She was dressed nice, makeup and hair done... he shouldn't have an issue. With quick, efficient movements, Rocco pulled her back and slammed her against the wall once more. A flare of pain lit up her scalp as she twisted her face to prevent her nose from breaking against the plaster. Agony radiated from her cheek through her head, creating an instant headache that left her moaning and unable to think past the hurt for a moment.

"On a public holiday when most things are shut? Tell me, pet. What shop were you planning on going to?"

Shit. She'd forgotten all about it being Australia Day. No lawyer would be open until tomorrow. The club would also be closed, but the bar would still be open later on tonight.

"The supermarket's open, I was just going to grab a few things."

"Bullshit. You were going to go find that bald bastard weren't you? You've been flirting with that animal and now he's got it in his head that you're his. Unfortunately, my bosses think he's right. All of that adds up to me losing you. How the fuck am I meant to run this place without you here? Did you think of that? No. You just went happily around flirting with any male who glanced your way. Well, never again. And you won't be going anywhere unless I let you."

Rachel tried to follow his ranting but she couldn't work out what the hell he was on about. He owned the bar, he was the damn boss. Her heart clenched at his mention of her running this place. Guess she now knew why he kept her around despite the fact he was sleeping with other women.

As he continued to carry on about how somehow everything was going wrong and it was all her fault, he loosened his grip on her hair, enabling her to pull free. Using every ounce of energy she had, she bolted out the door and sprinted down the hall.

"Run all you like, pet. You won't get out, all the doors are locked. Since I'm going to have to do your jobs tonight I need to work, but don't worry. I'll find you later and we'll finish this discussion."

He yelled after her as she skidded her way up the stairs.

Like hell he'd find her later. She needed to find the backbone she'd somehow lost since meeting Rocco, and get herself the hell away from him.

It was an hour later that she slumped into the lounge in defeat. Rocco had indeed locked every damn door, and all the windows on the ground level. Windows on the upper level were all too small for her to climb out if she broke one. Stupid old buildings and their daft design. How could she get out? She moved over to grab her handbag then upended it on the coffee table. Pawing through all the junk she'd accumulated, she didn't stop until she found her phone. Quickly, she returned everything else to her bag before she sat back once more. She brought up the contact information and sat staring at the ten numbers that could potentially save her.

Kit had promised her that her and her team could get her free from Rocco when she'd programed her number into Rachel's phone. She'd told her call if she ever needed her help. She knew deep down that team would include, if not led, by Xander. Was it worth the risk? Well, if Rocco wasn't even going to allow her to leave the apartment, she didn't have a lot to lose did she? With the way his fits of temper were worsening, she'd be dead by his hands before long. A shudder ran through her entire being. How had it gotten to this? How had she not seen it coming?

Shaking the thoughts free, she focused on the number once more as pressed the connect button to ring Kit. Lifting the phone to her ear, excitement bubbled in her tummy. She'd done it. She'd made the first move.

"Hey, you've reached Kit. I'm probably out putting water on a fire someplace so leave a message and I'll get back to you."

With a curse she hung up and flopped back on the couch defeated. Again. Dammit. She'd have to try again later, she didn't dare risk leaving a message and have her call back when Rocco was near.

With a roll of her shoulders, Kit pushed into the women's change rooms at the Hobart firehouse. It was still peak fire season, combine that with the public holiday and she should have predicted it was going to be a busy day. No way would she and the twins get to Classic Convicts tonight the way things were going. Why so many idiots spent their time off on a hot day lighting up shit they shouldn't was beyond her. Shrugging out of her turnout gear, she snatched a cloth to wipe the soot off her face. Then she grabbed her phone to see if anyone had reached out.

"Fuck."

Missed call from the number she'd grabbed off Rachel's phone. Without skipping a beat, she hit the call back button and waited as it rung.

"Hello?"

Yep, only one woman Kit knew with a British accent.

"Hey Rach, sorry I missed your call. I was out at a fire. What's up?"

"It's bad, Kit. He's lost the bloody plot. He's locked me in, I can't leave."

A flash of anger surged through her. "Why the hell did he do that?"

"Last night I, uh—last night I caught him shagging one of the girls and later when I pulled him about it, he uh, he decided I'd make a good punching bag. Fuck. He denied sleeping with her, even though I saw them, then he wanted to have sex. I said no way and he started laying into me. I know I have to leave. Even if I end up back in England, I have to get out of here. But this morning when I tried to go, I couldn't. He's locked all the damn doors."

Holy shit. Kit wasn't sure what the fuck to do. They'd lose precious information and the chance to take out a major Trigger player if Rachel called in the cops, but if Rocco got taken in, Xander could get Rachel without bloodying his hands.

"Have you rung the police? There's laws against the shit Rocco's pulling."

Rachel's voice wobbled a little as she answered. "There's no use. To keep his club running, he's made sure to gather dirt on several cops. If I rung and got one of them, they'd run straight to him and he'd rain all sorts of hell down on me. I can't risk it."

Kit cursed, low and harsh.

"Let me call my team and get something sorted. I might not be able to make it, Rach. I'm on call, if there's another fire I have to go, but my boys will never cause you harm. Do you hear me? You can trust them all, and I guarantee none of my team is in that bastard's pocket."

"How can you be sure? They've been coming into the

club for months!"

"I know you met Xander and you know we're on the same team. The boys have been going to the club to have Xander's back in keeping you safe. He cares about you."

"How can he? He doesn't know me! I can't handle any man's attention. Not now. Fuck, I'm not even sure I should rely on you! I can't trust my own judgment anymore. If I screwed up with Rocco so badly, who's to say I haven't with everyone else?"

Kit growled as fury blazed within her. "Listen to me, Rachel. You can trust me, and you can trust my team. Rocco is a bastard who abuses you. I'm sure he started subtly, then worked up to violence. Think back. Then think about me. All I've done is be your friend. I've never asked you to do anything, other than let me help you."

"Shit, he's coming. I gotta go."

"Rach, get in the bedroom and wedge a chair under that doorknob. Don't you let him lay a hand on you again."

Before Kit could say a word more the call cut off and she barely resisted the temptation to throw her phone across the room. Fuck! She needed to ring Xander, and Jake, to check on the arrival of their second team. Once she told Xander what Rocco had done, he'd lose his shit and run in after her. She doubted Jake would lock him down a second time. Their Alpha was just as worried for Rachel's safety as the rest of them.

Staring at her phone she was torn on who to ring. Jake was her Alpha, but Xander was the leader of the team. What to do, what to do...

Since Sophie woke that morning, she hadn't been able to shake the feeling that something big and bad was going to happen soon. She'd spoken with Jake late last night and knew of their plans to rescue Rachel tonight, so she supposed that was why she felt out of sorts. But unlike her husband and mate, Sophie didn't pick up on other's emotions. Jake had always had strong empathic senses, to the point it made him physically ill to be around someone experiencing extreme emotions. His ability to cope with the bombardment was decreasing as he got older too. Maybe when he returned from Hobart she would encourage him to hand over his duties as Alpha to their son. Dominic had been trained for the role and now that he was settled with his own mate, more than ready for the responsibility.

A shiver racked her body and for some reason Sophie couldn't push the dark cloud within her aside. Unsure how to deal with this strange sense of impending doom, she headed to her phone to ring Jake. It was still an hour or so before he'd head off with the team to Classic Convicts. Hopefully, hearing his voice would soothe her raw nerves. Of course, feeling his arms around her would work even better, but that wasn't going to happen today. She'd managed to make it down to Hobart most weekends to spend time with her mate, but she was used to having him around all the time and the weeks without him dragged on like she couldn't believe.

The phone only rung once before Jake picked it up.

"Sophie my love, it's so good to hear your voice."

His voice sounded strained and her heart ached for her mate.

"How is everything going? You all set for tonight?"

"Xander and Sean are loading up the vehicles as we wait for Dominic and his team to arrive. Kit and the twins are still down at the station. They had a call out earlier. Hopefully they return in time, but we can't wait for them. We need to get this done and over with."

Sophie recalled Jake telling her they hoped to be able to enter and snatch Rachel while Rocco was busy in the bar. Then, once it was closed, they would go in and deal with him. With the public holiday, the club wouldn't be opening tonight so there were less people around.

"Do you really believe it will be so simple to get her out? I have a bad feeling, love."

She clearly heard his sigh. "I do too. I doubt it will be as easy as we hope, but one way or the other we will get Rachel free and deal with Rocco. I hated having to lock Xander down last night, but he would have gotten himself caught if he'd gone in. I could sense how manic he was to find his mate. He wasn't thinking rationally at all. Today he's better. I'm not sensing any of that craziness I was last night.

"The upside is, we should all be back home tonight or tomorrow. Once we blow our cover at Classic Convicts we can return to Rosebery to continue our research on Triggers. No doubt the ones with Rocco will scatter, but it's too dangerous to leave Rachel there."

Sophie understood why they had to go in, but it didn't mean she had to like it. Snow leopard shifters were peaceful by nature. They were also protectors, and even if Rachel wasn't Xander's mate, they would never leave a woman where they knew she was being abused.

"How is Xander holding up?"

"He's hurting, there's no doubt about that, but so far he's holding it together to lead the team. Like I said before, I had to lock him down last night to prevent him running off to save her. But once we started the team meeting I could lift it as he settled back into his role with the team. After how he's handled himself with this mission, I have every confidence he'll be able to lead them to great success on other Trigger runs."

"Yes, well, having his mate on the line is certainly a pressure he'll hopefully never have to deal with again."

"Once Xander has mated her and brought her in to our world, we'll set about training her. Give her some skills to help in the future. Assuming she goes with Xander and the team, she'll need to learn to fight and be aware of her surroundings to remain safe."

Sophie's heart rate tripled when Jake abruptly stopped speaking and voices got louder in the background.

"What's happened?"

"Kit's rung Xander. Rachel called her. Rocco has her locked inside the building. Shit, I'm sorry Soph, I have to go."

Sophie's whole body trembled and her mouth was dry but she forced words from her tight throat.

"Please be careful. I have a bad feeling about tonight."

"You know I'm always careful. Love you, Soph and I'll call you when it's all over."

"Love you too, Jake. Go take care of things, then return to me."

She'd barely finished talking when the line was cut. A sob tore from her throat. She detested violence, and if nothing else, she could guarantee tonight would bring that. She sent a silent prayer that Jake and all their leap members returned safely from tonight's raid. She knew how bloodthirsty Trigger could be. She'd seen it first hand when they'd nearly wiped out her hometown. Thankfully Jake had arrived with a team in time to save her and a few others.

A solid knock on the door pulled her free of her depressing thoughts and she wiped her tears away as she went to see who it was. When she pulled open the door she stumbled against the wall.

"Choden, why are you here?"

The original shifter was nearly two hundred and seventy years old and a complete mystery to everyone. He still looked like a thirty-year-old Buddhist monk, always wearing the orange robe they were known for. He also had a habit of turning up right before he was needed. It was an omen she didn't want tonight.

"You feel it too, don't you? That tonight is going to be bad."

He clasped her hands in his. "Yes, Sophie. I do. But I cannot answer your questions about what will come to pass. It has not yet been decided. Decisions are still to be made before the night's course will be set in stone."

Chapter Six

For at least half an hour after Rocco stopped pounding on the door, Rachel stayed huddled in the far corner of the bedroom. Her heart was still racing, but had settled somewhat since she first wedged that chair under the door handle. Amazing that something so simple had kept her safe. Why hadn't she thought of doing it before? A shudder ran through her. Because no matter how long she kept him out, at some point she had to leave the room and face him. With the way his fits of rage had been increasing lately, she wasn't looking forward to the inevitable confrontation.

How could she get free? Kit had said she'd send her team in, but as far as Rachel knew, Kit was the only woman and wouldn't be able to make it if she was out fighting a fire. Rachel wasn't ready to trust any male, even one that Kit vouched for. Deep down she knew she could trust Kit, especially after their conversation and her tip about the chair. It was clear the woman wanted to help her, she was just unable to right now.

Rachel stilled as a crazy idea came to her.

"That might just work."

Not giving herself time to think about it further, she rose from her hiding spot and crept over to the door. She was certain Rocco had gone to open up the bar but she didn't want to risk racing out and landing in his lap. As quietly as possible, she removed the chair and opened the door to peek out. Her shoulders dropped in relief when she discovered no sign of Rocco. She repeated the process with the apartment's front door before she went flying down the back stairs as fast as she could without slipping.

When she reached HoHaven she paused a moment to listen for any sign that someone was down there. When all she heard was silence she slipped into the store room, grabbed the closest bottle of alcohol, then bolted down to Rocco's office. Using the spare key she'd nabbed from upstairs, she unlocked the door and shut herself in. It was the work of a moment to find a lighter and a pack of cigarettes. The man kept them all over the place.

Quickly she scrunched up paper and left it around his ashtray before making a trail over to the filing cabinet, which she opened an inch or so, hoping it would be enough for the flames to take hold. Opening the bottle, she poured the clear liquid over the crap in the cabinet then in a trail over to the desk. Leaving the bottle on its side near the ashtray, she prayed it would look like an accident of a lit cigarette and a tipped over bottle of vodka when the fire was put out.

Nerves had her hands trembling and she took a deep breath to steady herself enough to light a cigarette. Once she got the thing lit, she went over to open the door before heading back to the desk. Then she tossed it in the ashtray and she jumped back. She didn't pour the vodka into the ashtray, hoping it would give her a minute to get out of the room. As she sprinted out of the room she heard the whoosh and felt a blast of heat.

Perfect.

When she got to the back stairwell, she pulled out her phone and called emergency to report the fire—and the fact the exits were all locked so she was stuck inside. After the operator assured her help was on the way, she ended the call and moved toward the end of the hallway. She glanced over her shoulder briefly and seeing an orange glow in Rocco's office doorway, she ran up the stairs.

She'd done it. Kit had to come help her now. Rachel was sure once Kit saw the address she'd rush to help her. A frown crept over her face and she stumbled up a step. What if she was somewhere else at a fire and couldn't come? Had she just lit her own death trap? She shook her head. Even if it wasn't Kit, someone would come to put out the fire and Rocco would be forced to unlock the doors. When he did, she'd be free to leave.

Rubbing her still-aching ribs, Rachel wondered if the firefighters would arrive before Rocco discovered the fire. He'd no doubt fly into a rage when he did find out about it. At the very least his office was toast. She paused and tilted her head to listen. Why weren't there sounds of a fire alarm? The place might be old, but surely it was up to code? Had Rocco been stupid enough to turn them off? On top of locking the fire escapes, he was going to be seeing some heavy fines when this was all over.

She licked her dry lips at that thought and sent up a

silent prayer that help arrived before the fire grew too big to stop. Not paying attention to her surroundings, she didn't see Rocco until she ran into him. With a gasp she pushed against his chest to look up at his face. Ice slid down her spine as she stared into his furious expression.

"Any reason why you're not where I left you, pet?"

His falsely calm voice didn't fool her for a moment and sure enough, before she could respond he'd wrapped his hand around her bicep in a bruising grip to drag her up the final steps to the apartment.

"I just went downstairs for a drink, that's all. I knew you didn't want me in the bar so I quickly went down to the club. I didn't see anyone, Rocco."

She quickly realized that trying to placate him wasn't going to work, as with a wince, the breath was knocked from her when he slammed her back against the wall. With his fingers firmly wrapped around her throat, she tried to slow her panicked breathing. He was pushing hard enough she could feel it on her windpipe. Raising her hands, she tried to pull him away from her neck, but with a growl he had her wrists against the wall above her head with his other hand. As tears pricked her eyes, she struggled to get free. At the same time a swirl of smoke came through the doorway, Rachel heard sirens nearing.

Rocco shook her against the wall. "What the fuck did you do?"

Feeling brave with help so close she glared at him as she spoke.

"What I had to. I will not be your punching bag. You

can't keep me locked up to abuse at your whim. Not anymore."

"You stupid bitch. You've no—"

His words were cut off by a loud bang followed by Roger's deep masculine voice bellowing up the stairs.

"Boss! The club's up in flames. I've cleared the bar and am about to go myself. You need to get out of here fast before the whole place goes up."

Rachel winced. Her hope for a small fire contained to Rocco's office hadn't happened. She'd not fully thought through lighting flames so close to so much alcohol. At least Roger would clear out everyone from the bar, and the club had been empty so at this point it was only her and Rocco at risk from the flames.

Just as Rocco focused on her again a loud crash shuddered through the building followed by a man's booming voice.

"Rachel! Where are you?"

Relief had her closing her eyes. Help was here. The sirens were still getting closer, but that voice was Xander's. She was certain.

With a sharp gasp her eyes snapped open when Rocco released her to back-hand her hard enough she ended up across the room. Cradling her aching jaw she whimpered as Rocco stormed over to her with wild rage flaring in his gaze.

Perhaps help hadn't arrived in time after all.

Fury radiated from Xander and if Jake didn't put all his

effort into focusing on keeping the emotion out, he was going to be physically ill for ages. But he couldn't afford to let his weakness hamper him this afternoon.

"What did Kit say exactly?"

"That I was right about Rocco bashing my mate last night, and this morning Rachel woke to discover she'd been locked in the building. She hung up on Kit because he was coming after her again. Kit told her to get in a room and jam the door with a chair, but that won't stop him for long. I need to get to her now. Who knows what else the bastard will do to my mate."

Guilt sliced deeply into Jake. Things had gone from bad to worse far quicker than he'd anticipated, and all of it could have been prevented if only he'd allowed Xander to go in last night. Of course, allowing the young shifter to go rushing in high on emotion could have potentially ended worse than what they were dealing with now. He shook his head to clear his thoughts. All the 'what ifs' and 'if onlys' weren't going to do anyone a lick of good. He needed to focus.

He followed Xander and wasn't surprised when Jessie and Sean joined them by the time they'd made it to the front door.

"Xander? Give me the keys, *amigo*. I'll get us there faster."

Jake winced as without a word Xander tossed to keys to Jessie. Jessie's rally skills would no doubt have them making good time, but this was a street car with no racing harnesses to hold them in. He wasn't looking forward to being tossed around on their journey, but he wasn't going to say a word. He could live with a few bruises, especially if it meant they got to Classic Convicts in time to save Rachel. Jake managed to get his seatbelt buckled seconds before Jessie took off like he'd been shot out of a gun.

In the confined space of the vehicle Jake focused on his breathing to prevent the emotions overwhelming him. Xander was radiating desperation and fear, Jessie was awash with cool determination. He was in his driving zone, which meant the man had pushed most of his emotions aside, something Jake was grateful for. Sean, who was seated in the back next to Jake was putting out fury. Sean had been close to Nick, who Trigger had killed less than three months ago. His need for revenge on Trigger was fueling his every move on this mission.

All these emotions swirled around the vehicle and continuously bombarded Jake's sensitive empathetic scenes. Add to that his own guilt, worry and anger and Jake was on the edge of collapsing in agony. But he couldn't afford for that to happen. His leap needed him, and the last thing this team needed was to be distracted by him needing help.

His next deep breath was cut short when Xander's phone rang once more.

"Yeah, Kit."

Jake focused on Xander's expression. With how this situation was going, he doubted Kit would be ringing with good news.

"Are you kidding me? For fuck's sake. Okay, we're

only a couple minutes out. See you soon."

Xander hung up and without turning his face away from where he stared out the windscreen, he spoke in a hard biting tone. "Classic Convicts is on fire. Kit and the twins, along with a crew from the Hobart Firehouse, are on the way but she's not sure how long it's been burning. She couldn't call until they were en route, so it was called in as long ago as fifteen minutes by the time the alarm went through to the station, they kitted up and headed out."

Jake closed his eyes as he fought the bile that rose up his throat. Could this situation get any worse? He shook his head. No, he refused to say it out loud. They didn't need to tempt fate like that.

Minutes later they skidded to stop outside Classic Convicts to the sight of a dozen or so people running from the main bar's entrance. Glancing down the side alley he saw smoke was pouring out through the cracks in the door that led down to HoHaven. Just as he stepped free of the car the old wooden door burst into flame.

"Fuck!"

Xander took off toward the door that, according to the floor plan they'd seen, opened to a staircase that led to the apartment upstairs. Jake wasted no time in running after him. He caught up to Xander as the man kicked the door in with one well-placed kick.

As soon as they were both inside, Xander bellowed up the stairs. "Rachel! Where are you?"

Jake inhaled deeply, trying to catch any scents that might give away where Rachel or Rocco were. He didn't think anyone else would have stuck around with the fire, but he couldn't risk someone coming up behind them while Xander was preoccupied.

"They're upstairs. He just hit her."

With a nod, Jake followed Xander across the foyer to the stairs. He didn't doubt Xander's statement—with the man's sensitive hearing, he would have heard when flesh met flesh. As Xander put his foot on the bottom stair he froze. Jake stopped scanning and focused up at what had caught the other man's attention. *Oh shit.* Rocco was a dead man walking.

At the top of the stairs Rocco had a nearly unconscious Rachel by the hair as he held a kitchen knife against her pale throat. Looked like he'd hit her more than once, unless the injuries were from what he'd done the night before. Bloody hell, he should have let Xander come earlier. They'd decided the cover of night would help them to go unnoticed but now, Jake didn't think that should have been the priority. No woman deserved to be treated as Rachel had obviously been.

"I hear you think this is yours?"

Jake winced when Rocco shifted the knife away and shook her. Rachel moaned, but her eyes stayed closed.

"Careful Xander. You rush up to them, he could kill her before you get there. Even with your speed."

Jake spoke low so only Xander would hear him. He had to pull him back from following his mating instincts to rush in to rescue his mate, and he couldn't risk locking him down in this situation because he may need to move quickly to avoid an attack. Xander gave him a slight nod before he spoke to Rocco.

"I don't think, I know."

Rocco laughed, like the bastard thought he was going to walk away from this the victor. "You cats are all so predictable. All we need to do is find your mate and you'll do whatever we want."

A deep growl vibrated the room. "So you finally figured out what I am. If Trigger trained you at all, you know I'll never let anyone live if they lay a hand on my mate."

"Oh, Xander, trust me. I've laid more than a hand on her." He lowered the knife down to Rachel's belly where he hooked it under her shirt and easily sliced the material up the center. The fabric fell open revealing Rachel's bruised ribs and her plain black bra. The smug bastard ran the backs of his knuckles over the swell of Rachel's right breast—thankfully keeping the blade away from her skin. "I've been laying all sorts of things all over her for over a year and I'm still here, alive and well. I think that might just be an empty threat."

Jake grabbed Xander's shoulder as he went to move up the stairs. "Easy, son."

A loud bang from downstairs shook the building and with a curse, Rocco dropped the knife to shove Rachel down the stairs. Her scream echoed around the small space and the terror pouring off her had Jake gagging.

Xander leapt up to catch her and Jake didn't watch to see if he was successful. He knew without a doubt, he would. No, Jake kept his gaze on Rocco, who'd stood still a moment to watch Rachel fall, but now was running down a hallway. No doubt to another exit. Jake couldn't let him escape. Not after all the harm the bastard had caused.

He pushed past Xander and was bounding up the stairs when the younger man called out.

"Wait! Jake don't. The fire is getting bigger and this place is unstable, we have to get out of here. We'll catch him outside."

"No, we won't. You take care of your mate and let me handle Rocco."

Not giving him time to respond, Jake turned and sprinted after Rocco—who, hopefully, thanks to his years of heavy smoking and no exercise, wasn't that far ahead of him. Unlike firefighting boots, his sneakers did nothing to prevent the heat radiating up from the blaze burning below, which made his feet sweat uncomfortably. If the fire was already burning this hot, he needed to deal with Rocco quickly and get the hell out of the building.

Rocco glanced over his shoulder, then with a curse, stopped and spun to face Jake. Considering the idiot was Trigger, he should have known from the get-go he'd never outrun a shifter. Jake slowed to carefully prowl up the hallway. Some of the floorboards were beginning to buckle from the heat, and it wouldn't take much to fall through them.

"Well well, if it isn't the all-powerful Alpha. When I bring you in, I'll be the favorite. Might just be worth all I've lost."

"Oh, you won't be taking me anywhere. You're done

with hurting anyone, shifter or human."

The bastard laughed as he reached into his pocket. "And who's going to stop me? You? Look at yourself. You're pale and about to pass out. Pathetic."

True, he was feeling the weight of all the strong emotions he'd been surrounded with all day but he was more than capable of taking out this piece of shit. Calling on his leopard, he grinned as his vision filled with a blue glow. His cat would rip out Rocco's throat and be able to get out of the building in minutes. A moment before the shift was complete he saw Rocco pull out a Taser and line it up on him.

Fool. His leopard would withstand the jolt of electricity easily. But before Jake could fully shift to his feline form, Rocco pulled the trigger and when the pins connected with the energy field surrounding him things went to hell.

Agony took over his whole being as, still in human form, he flew backward with enough force that when he landed he went straight through the weakened floor and crashed down to land in a heap on the level below. He was in so much pain his muscles wouldn't move, even when he felt the intense heat that meant the flames were close to licking his skin.

He heard heavy footsteps, like those of firefighters in full BA gear, but his eyesight wouldn't clear. The world was foggy and he couldn't make out more than vague shapes. Blurry yellow shapes were racing toward him when he heard an ominous crack from above. Still unable to move his arms or legs, he glanced up to see what must be a floor support from the upper level come swinging down straight at him. Another explosion of pain ricocheted through him and he used his last ounce of energy to send out a thought to his mate. His love and an apology that he wouldn't be coming home tonight after all. Then his world was inky black and silent.

But at least he didn't hurt anymore.

Chapter Seven

Even using all of his shifter speed, Xander wasn't fast enough and he winced when Rachel cried out as her shoulder slammed against the wall. Then, everything around him ceased to exist the moment he caught her. She was a sweet weight in his arms and in her weakened state, she didn't fight him as he'd anticipated she would. Instead she nuzzled her face against his chest and wrapped a fist in his t-shirt to hang on to him. *Like I'd ever let her go.*

Jake pushing past him pulled his attention from Rachel. He couldn't see Rocco and Jake was clearly prepared to rush off after him.

"Wait! Jake, don't. The fire is getting bigger and this place is unstable, we have to get out of here. We'll catch him outside."

"No we won't. You take care of your mate and let me handle Rocco."

Xander wanted to pull the older man back. He knew Jake was feeling guilty about Rachel's injuries but running off half-cocked through a burning building wasn't going to fix anything. He needed to get Rachel to safety so he could come back and help Jake. Spinning on his heel, he rushed out of the building to find that the fire trucks and ambulance had arrived. Unfortunately, it wasn't Adele's bus so Rachel would no doubt end up at Hobart's hospital. Hopefully her injuries weren't anything needing surgery and she'd be released within hours so he wouldn't be separated from her long.

Following the medic's instructions, he carefully laid Rachel down on the gurney, peeling her fingers from where she was clutching his shirt with a death grip.

"Shh, it's okay Rachel. Let the medics check you out, okay? I need to go let the others know that Jake is still in the building but I'll be right back. I promise."

With his heart aching at the sorrow that had filled Rachel's eyes that she was struggling to keep open, Xander made his way over to the truck. Quickly locating the captain on shift, he jogged over to him, raising his hand as he neared.

"Hey, Xander. What are you doing here?"

"Jake's in there. You need to tell your guys to look for Jake."

The man jerked with a shock, but quickly lifted his radio to tell all units in the building to keep a look out for Jake.

"Coming out with him now. Need medic."

The tinny voice that came back over the radio had him wincing. Then his heart stopped and his lungs refused to work when, moments later, Joel exited the house with a limp and bloodied Jake in his arms.

"No."

His voice was hoarse and the word sounded so stupid. Like he could undo this night and start over with a simple *no*? Shaking off his shock, he bolted back to the ambulance. A second bus had pulled up and Joel rushed Jake over to it before Xander could get there. He tried to hone his hearing into the medics working on his Alpha but he simply couldn't focus enough to do it. He was worried about Rachel, and scared shitless that Jake was going to die.

"What's going on?"

Kit appeared at his side, in full turnout gear, ash smudged over her face and a look of desperation in her gaze.

"I don't know. Were you with Joel when he found him?"

"Yeah, he was conscious but wasn't moving after coming through the floor. A beam came down on him. We were almost to him but couldn't get there in time to prevent the hit."

Xander squeezed his eyes shut as agony assailed him. "I told him not to go. Dammit."

Kit's strong grip on his shoulder had him looking his leap sister in the eye.

"Xander, this isn't your fault. You hear me? Whatever the outcome, this is not your fault."

"It feels like it, Kit. This is my team, my mission. And I have my mate and Alpha in ambulances. No Triggers taken out. It's hardly a success."

Kit gave his shoulder another squeeze, but didn't say a word. What could she say? This whole situation was a cluster fuck that couldn't be reversed. Then she turned and jogged back over to the truck to continue fighting the fire. Classic Convicts was going to be nothing more than a pile of rubble by morning.

Glancing over at the bus where Jake was, he took in all the medics attempting to stabilize the man. He sent up a silent prayer that Jake would pull through as he turned back to his mate.

"Shit." He rushed over there as the driver shut the rear door. "Can I get a lift the hospital with you?"

"You family?"

He wanted to say yes, but if he did and she'd said it was her fiancé who'd beaten her, he'd end up locked up and further away from her.

"I'm the off duty firefighter that pulled her out of that deathtrap."

The guy nodded. "I can't let you ride in the back with her, only family allowed to do that, but if you want, you can jump up front with me."

"Thanks, man."

He'd have preferred sit next to her, but he knew this was as good as he was going to get.

Rachel kept her eyes closed as she lay in the ambulance. She couldn't stand the looks of pity from the medics. She knew her body told a pretty clear tale of what she'd been through. Every bump in the road jolted through her, making all her injuries ache. But the truly stupid thing that had her completely baffled was the fact she knew without a doubt that Xander sat up the front of the vehicle and having him close eased her pain.

Madness. Total madness.

The ambulance sliding to a stop pulled her from her introspection and she forced her eyes to open when the gurney she was on began to move. Naturally, the first thing she saw was Xander's dirt streaked face. He stared at her as though he couldn't stand the idea she was hurt. But why would he even care? They were strangers. All she knew of him was his name, occupation and what he looked like. As far as she knew, he didn't know any more about her than she did him.

She continued to frown up at him as she was wheeled into the hospital and the medics moved her to a hospital bed and gave the nurses a report on her status. Her heart sunk at the list. How had she not seen what Rocco was capable of sooner? Surely there had been signs. Did she not see them, or had she subconsciously known but ignored it?

One thing she was sure of was that she didn't need another man in her life. She was now free and clear of Rocco and had no intention of getting trapped ever again. Plenty of women stayed single and had great lives. She closed her eyes as tears pricked them. What was she going to do? She had nothing. No home, no possessions. Not even her passport. Not that she wanted to go back home to England.

A sob tore from her throat and her body began to shake as she cried uncontrollably. She attempted to roll to her side, wanting to curl into a ball but her injured ribs screamed in pain and forced her to remain flat on her back.

"Shh baby girl, you're going to hurt yourself if you don't settle down."

Xander's voice was rough with emotion and his big work-roughened hands cupped her face as he pressed a kiss to her forehead. With a jerk, she pulled away from his gentle touch. She couldn't handle dealing with him right now. With the way she was falling apart, she was likely to forget her resolve to be an island and cling to the man. She couldn't risk it.

"Leave me alone! Just go away!"

She stopped screaming when a cold palm held down her arm. She whimpered as a needle was efficiently slid into the vein at her inner elbow. Her mind was a mess; she couldn't focus on any one thought. Panic rose and she struggled to breathe past it all, then her thoughts cleared and her body relaxed. Whatever they'd pumped into her system started working its magic and she closed her eyes to float away from everything and everybody.

When she next opened her eyes it was to a private hospital room. But she wasn't alone, there was a man sitting beside her bed. She'd never seen him before and he was clearly some kind of monk. He wore red and gold robes like she'd seen on documentaries about the Tibetan culture and had a cleanly shaven head, just like Xander, who she sensed was just outside her room's door. Mentally shaking her head, she quickly pushed thoughts of him away and focused on the man before her who was simply sitting there, looking like he was meditating or something. She frowned as she attempted to sit up. With a kind smile, the man reached over and handed her the control to the bed.

"I believe you will find you are still too weak to sit on your own, child. Make use of the bed to assist you."

Her mouth was beyond dry and her throat felt as though it had been lined with sandpaper. With a trembling hand she raised the bed then reached for the glass of water that sat on the tray beside her. When the cold liquid hit her parched tongue, she closed her eyes a moment to enjoy the sensation. Once she was confident she could speak without croaking too badly, she licked her lips and focused on the man still calmly watching her.

"Who are you?"

"My name is Choden Sangye, and I have come to help you."

Rachel tilted her head as she frowned. Help her? What could this monk, who didn't look a day older than thirty, possibly do for her? As far as she knew, monks were peaceful men, so offering to take out Rocco probably wasn't what he meant.

"I am not nearly as young as you think, Rachel Bell, but I'll get to that later."

Before he could continue, she interrupted him. "How do you know my name? And what I was thinking?"

He simply smiled gently at her. "It is what everyone thinks upon meeting me if they do not have prior knowledge of who I am. And I know much about you—I suspect my knowledge on the subject, is, in fact, greater than your own. But that's for later. I believe starting from the beginning is always best. Will you allow me to tell you a story? If it would make you more comfortable I can call Xander in."

Rachel couldn't help it, she scoffed. "Xander rarely makes me more comfortable. Mostly he just confuses the hell out of me."

Choden chuckled. "Yes, I suppose at this point he does. But soon you will understand why he has been so determined to protect you. Will you allow me to call him in?"

Curiosity about what he wanted to tell her had her agreeing. She was in the safety of a hospital room with a button at her fingertips she could press to get the pair of them kicked out if she felt unsafe. And honestly, because she seemed to sense whenever he was close, he was equally distracting, whether he was out in the hallway or standing next to her.

Choden stood and made his way to the door where he said something too quietly for Rachel to hear. By the time he'd made his way back to his seat by her bed, Xander filled the doorway. He ran his gaze over her from head to toe, then stalked over to her side.

She couldn't pull her gaze away from him as he silently pulled a chair to the opposite side of her bed from Choden, then took her hand in his. She tensed when he lifted it to press a kiss to her inner wrist. Her heart skipped a beat and she tried to pull free, tugging a couple times before he released her with a soft sigh.

Choden cleared his throat. "This story starts long ago, back in the year 1759 when a Tibetan monk and his young prodigy realized the local population of snow leopards was rapidly declining. The monastery where these monks resided had a very close relationship with a leap of these leopards. One young monk had an especially close friendship with a particular animal. So, when the elder monk found a spell that would join the souls of a man and an animal together, the young monk volunteered himself and his snow leopard. Both men hoped that by combining the two it would create a shifter that would be capable of better protecting the leopards and the monks from any attacks.

"As the moon rose one night, they cast the spell, and initially it appeared to have worked as expected. The young monk and his snow leopard became one. But they did not realize that Halley's Comet passed overhead as they cast the spell. It was not until years later that they realized it was not only one single shifter created that night. The comet strengthened the spell and on top of the original shifter, there were also a mated pair of shifters conceived on each continent. Not only that, but Halley's Comet remains linked to the spell, and every time the comet passes over Earth, a new pair of shifters is conceived on each of the seven continents."

Rachel held her palm up for him to stop. His story had gone from past tense to present. Was he trying to imply this was a true story?

"What exactly are you trying to say here? That shape shifters are real? That this story is not simply some new fairytale I've never heard before?"

Choden held her gaze as he took her palm between his own. "My dear girl, it is all truth. And you are one of us."

She shook her head and pulled her hand free to wrap her arms around herself. "No. You lie. I've never turned into an animal. I think I would have noticed that-"

"Choden, her birthday is in March, not November, she can't possibly be a comet shifter. And if she were, she wouldn't be my mate. My parents are shifters."

Rachel turned her shocked gaze to Xander. He was in on this craziness? Was it all some elaborate scheme to lure her in to something?

Xander felt Rachel's rising panic but stayed focused on Choden. He didn't think him staring at her would help her process what was going on. He was still wrapping his mind around Rachel being one of them. He'd been certain she was human.

"No, she is not a Comet Shifter like your Kit and Jessie."

Rachel made a noise like she was choking and Xander spun toward her. Her gaze bounced between him and Choden. He reached to take her palms in his and her skin was cold and sweaty.

"Is everyone I've met in Tasmania in on this hoax?"

She believed they were attempting to trick her, his heart ached at her suffering.

"This is all truth, baby girl. I know it's a lot to take in but shifters are real. I am a shifter, as is Kit and all the men who used to come into Classic Convicts with me."

She hadn't pulled from his touch, but her gaze clearly told him she thought he was insane.

"Choden? Could I please ask you to guard the doorway so I can show Rachel my leopard?"

You didn't tell the original shifter to do anything. He was mysterious but kind, so Xander hoped he'd worded his request respectfully enough that the man would agree.

Choden dipped his head for a moment then made his way from the room. He closed the door and Xander didn't doubt he was standing against the other side. He gently placed Rachel's hands on the bed before he moved to the corner of the room where he'd have enough space to shift comfortably. Then he started to strip from his clothes.

"I have the same mind whether I'm animal or man, so don't be scared. Like me, my leopard would never do you any harm."

"And you're giving me a striptease why?"

Her eyes had darkened and her voice deepened as she watched him pull his shirt over his head.

"If we shift while wearing clothes, we shred them. It's why all of us keep a change of clothes in our cars, just in case we have to shift in a hurry."

Easily sensing how much Rachel was struggling with everything, he wasted no time stripping his lower half and calling on his leopard. He'd preen and flex his muscles for her some other time. As his vision turned blue from the glow of his change he saw her eyes go wide in shock. He blinked then tilted his head up to see her from his now lower height.

She had a palm pressed to her chest and her mouth hung open.

"Oh bloody hell, you really did it. You really turned into a damn cat!"

He padded toward her and when she stiffened, he started purring. Keeping his head lowered, trying to look less intimidating, he approached the bed. Not giving her time to panic, he slid his muzzle over her lap so he could rub the side of his head gently against her belly. He kept the contact light so he wouldn't aggravate any of her injuries.

She tentatively touched his ear and it automatically twitched at the contact. When she then sunk her whole hand into the fur on the top of his head he closed his eyes with a louder purr. Her touch was divine, no matter what form he was in.

He took a deep breath and could scent a trace of her leopard. In human form he'd never picked up on it, but his animal could clearly identify her as one of their kind. However, it was muted, as though it had been masked somehow. He needed to shift back so Choden could return and they could get some answers. *Hopefully.* Choden would only tell them what he believed they should know. If he deemed for some reason they didn't need to know something yet, he would happily withhold the information.

Reluctantly he stepped away from the bed and shifted back to his human form. Keeping his back turned to Rachel, he quickly put his jeans on, suddenly unsure what his mate would think of his body. With so much else to worry about, he didn't want to throw in her potential rejection of his manhood into the mix. He went to the door to call Choden back in before returning to his clothes to finish dressing.

"You're really a shape shifter. This is crazy!" She turned to stare at Choden. "I can't be like that. I've never changed. I'm pretty sure I'd remember if I'd ever gotten furry."

Xander tried to hold back his laugh, but a chuckle escaped when Choden gave her his trademark *I'm-being-patient-with-the-baby-shifter* smile. One Xander had received a time or two over the years.

Chapter Eight

"Your abilities have merely been hidden from you, but I assure you, you are one of us. You heal faster than normal, correct?"

Rachel's mind was still reeling with the images of Xander's sexy, naked body mixed in with him actually turning into a friggin' snow leopard. Now, this monk was trying to convince her she could change too.

"Sure. I've always recovered from small cuts and scrapes faster than my friends. But only a little quicker. It's not like I heal instantly or anything."

As evidenced by the fact she was stuck in a hospital bed thanks to her latest bout with Rocco.

"All your shifter abilities have been leashed. Here, allow me to free them."

Swallowing past a lump in her throat she tried to press herself away from Choden. What was he going to do with her? She reached for the call button to get a nurse but Xander took it then held her hand before she could press the damn thing.

"Please. Don't hurt me."

Her heart ached that she was already forced into being the victim again. This was why she never wanted to have a man in her life. Men equaled pain.

"My dear girl, I would never cause you harm. I protect all shifters. By releasing your abilities, you will heal from your current wounds much faster. It will also give you access to your leopard, which you can learn to use to keep yourself protected."

She still wasn't sure about it all and tried to push herself back away from the man's touch. But all she managed to do was end up pressed against Xander's torso as he stood blocking the other side of her bed. A whimper left her throat when Xander pulled her from the bed and into his arms, holding her easily against his torso. She pressed her palm over his heart. The feel of its strong beat comforted her.

"It's okay, baby girl. You can trust Choden. If you like, I can get Kit in here to vouch for him too?"

Rachel held Xander's deep brown gaze as she tried to work out what to do. She wasn't sure she trusted Xander, or Kit, fully yet. She did know, that with his strong arms around her, cradling her gently against his warm body, she felt safe. As though the world could throw anything at her and he'd block it from harming her.

She took a deep breath. She needed to be brave. If she wanted to no longer be that woman who got walked all over, then she needed to find her damn backbone.

"Okay."

Xander moved to sit on the mattress and helped her shift until she was lying against him, with her legs between his, and her back against his chest, facing out toward where

Choden was standing near them. With a kind smile, he pressed his palms to each side of her temple and began chanting in a language she didn't understand. Within moments, heat passed from his hands into her skull. With a gasp her vision went wavy then cleared to show a memory she'd forgotten all about.

Rachel sat quietly on the couch as she watched her parents talk with a strange woman. All three turned to look at her and she gripped her stuffed Tassie Devil. She loved her Tassie. Her friends at preschool all liked Bugs Bunny best, but not Rachel. She loved how Tassie spun really fast to escape what he didn't like.

The strange woman came to sit next to her and she wondered if she could spin fast enough to make the lady go away. She smelled funny and stared a lot. Mummy always said staring was rude. This woman's mummy must have not told her. Rachel's mother sat on her other side and Rachel crawled onto her lap.

"Can I go now, Mummy?"

"I'm sorry, darling. But we need you to stay."

"But I don't want to. I don't like her."

She squeezed Tassie tighter when her mother frowned.

"Now, Rachel. You know it's rude to say things like that. We're just going to play a little game. It won't take long, then you and Tassie can go play on the swings. Does that sound good?"

"Maybe this is a bad idea."

Her father sounded worried. Rachel blinked up at him as he moved to stand near her.

"Don't be silly, Neville. You know we need to do this. It's for her own protection. You want her to suffer under that bastard like the others?"

"Of course not! But she doesn't want this."

"She's just a child. She doesn't want to eat carrots either, but we don't let that stop us from making her eat them!"

Rachel screwed her nose up. She wished it would make them stop. Mushy carrots were disgusting. Did she look like a rabbit? No, she was a little girl. One that should be able to eat lollies and biscuits all day, not stupid carrots and vegetables. Catching her father's gaze, she batted her eyelids. That always worked when she wanted her way. She loved her daddy so much, he always gave in to her. Surely he'd save her from this strange woman who continued to sit there silently, staring at her.

"Sorry, pumpkin. But your mummy's right. You'll understand one day."

"Well, hopefully she'll never know."

The odd woman interrupted her parents. "So, are we doing this or not? I have other clients to attend to today."

Her mother moved Rachel so she faced the woman and her father pulled Tassie from her grip.

"No! Not Tassie! I need him."

"Not for the next couple minutes you don't. I promise I'll keep him safe for you."

With tears blurring her vision she looked up at the hard face of the woman. Fear had a wash of cold running down her back and she tried to wriggle out of her mother's arms.

"Just do it already. The longer we take, the more upset she'll get."

Her mother sounded angry but Rachel didn't care. She didn't want to play a game with this new woman. The lady reached forward and pressed a palm to each side of her head and Rachel cried out in pain.

With a jerk she blinked open her eyes to find herself back in the hospital room, wrapped in Xander's arms. She curled into his warmth and buried her face against his soft shirt. She needed a moment or two to process what she'd remembered. How had she forgotten that day? And what the hell happened after that woman touched her?

Keeping her fist wrapped in Xander's shirt she lifted her face to glare at Choden.

"Who the hell are you and what did you just do to me?"

She felt Xander tense beneath her as though she'd struck a nerve by speaking so harshly to the other man, but Rachel didn't give a damn. She wanted answers.

"I am the boy from the story. The original shifter—"

"Are you seriously telling me you're nearly three hundred years old?"

He nodded. "I am. Do not worry, you are not immortal. As the original shifter I am somewhat different. What I did was to lift the spell cast to dampen your abilities. I also sped up your healing. You are going to need all your strength for what is coming."

Realizing she was clinging to Xander like a kitten to a tree, she released his shirt and tried to roll off his body to stand up. Xander's arms tightened a moment before, with a low growl, he stood with her. He then carefully set her on her feet, pressed a kiss to the top of her head and stepped back from her. Testing her body, she paced the room, shocked when she didn't feel any of the aches and pains flare up as she moved. Too much had happened for her to process any of it. Her strange reaction to Xander, news shifters were not only real but she was apparently one of them, and now that the monk standing before her was in fact nearly three hundred years old, not thirty like she'd originally thought. It was all so beyond anything she'd ever even dreamed of, she wasn't sure where to start. So she decided starting with her body was as good a place as any.

"So I can now change into a cat?"

Choden nodded. "You will now be able to call on your snow leopard. As Xander demonstrated earlier, it is pain-free and immediate. You only need to focus on your feline self, and you will shift. It is the same process to then change back to human. However, it is only your physical self that changes. Any clothes you are wearing will be shredded."

Rachel frowned down at the hospital gown she wore. She didn't care if it got destroyed but she did care about flashing her naked self to the two men in the room.

"Think I'll try that one later."

Maybe she could get Kit to help her. She didn't want to end up stuck as a leopard because she panicked and couldn't change back.

"Choden, do you know why my abilities were blocked?"

His serene smile didn't give her hope that if he did in fact know why, that he would tell her.

"That is a tale your parents must tell you."

Rachel opened her mouth to argue but stopped herself. She got the feeling he wouldn't tell her no matter what she said or did. Then, a nurse knocked and entered, ending all shifter conversation.

"Oh, you're up and around. Guess you weren't kidding when you said you healed quickly. Let me go grab the doctor and we'll get you discharged so you can get out of here."

The nurse left as swiftly as she came, but Rachel couldn't move. She could barely breathe. Where would she go? She had nothing but her mobile phone. She had no money for a hotel. Xander's fingers gently wiping her cheeks snapped her attention to him.

"I've got nowhere to go."

Her voice was whisper quiet and she barely heard herself, but Xander heard her.

"You can come stay with me."

As though someone ran an ice cube down her spine, she jerked away from his touch shaking her head.

"No. I can't. I can't do that. Not again."

Her heart clenched when Xander winced then folded his arms defensively across his chest.

"I am not Rocco, Rachel. I'm your mate, I'd never hurt you. In fact, I'm the one that'll make sure no one ever hurts you again."

Momentarily distracted from her homelessness issue

she glared at Xander.

"Mate? What, like some fated pairing is why you've been following me around for months? Did you know it was his jealousy of you that turned him violent?"

Anger flared bright. It was all Xander's fault that Rocco lost his shit and started hitting her. A niggling feeling deep within her wouldn't go away, but she pushed it aside. Being angry felt good. She had so much bottled up, she needed to blow some of it off.

With his jaw clenched, Xander took a couple deep breaths through his nose to calm down. He was fairly certain his mate didn't truly blame him, but he couldn't be sure.

"I know because I'm here, it's easy to blame me. But it's not my fault Rocco is a bastard. A few rare shifters have an extra enhancement. I'm one of them. You want to know what my gift is? I have extremely sensitive hearing. That first time I came in I heard what he said to you, how he treated you. He'd been abusing you long before he raised a fist. And I know men like that, anything will set them off. I refuse to be your scapegoat in this."

"Why? Because we're mates?"

Silently he watched his little spitfire. She'd been dealt a lot of information in a very short amount of time, add into that she'd lost her home and everything she owned. She was no doubt scared, confused and her anger was winning out. He strode over to her and wrapped her in his arms before she had time to protest.

"All shifters have one predestined mate. Their perfect other half. It's not just fate saying two people will be together, it's aligning two souls that were born to complement each other. When you turned twenty-one, on the ninth of March 2007, I started dreaming of you. That's what happens to all male shifters when their mate turns twenty-one. At first I only saw glimpses of your face and hair, then over time I saw all of you and heard your voice. By the time I heard your accent, I'd also seen places around you and knew you were somewhere in Australia. I'd guessed the East Coast and had planned on searching for you after this mission."

Rachel's breathing had increased and she shook her head against his chest.

"This is insane. I will admit there is some kind of weird attraction happening between us, but I'm not ready for it. Any of it. Rocco took so much, I can't risk getting involved with another man. I need to find myself again. I lost who I am somehow."

She'd lifted her face to stare up at him and the sorrow in her gaze broke his heart. But he heard what she was saying. He couldn't fight her on this and win, at least not yet.

"If I may interrupt? I believe I have a solution."

Rachel jerked at the same moment Xander did. Clearly she'd also forgotten that Choden was still in the room with them.

"What would that be?"

He winced at the way her voice cracked as she spoke. How he wished he could just take her away from the world and keep her safe and protected.

"There is an older couple with a spare room in their home in Rosebery. Jennifer is a shifter and a psychiatrist. I believe she would be able to help you adjust to your new-found abilities, along with being able to explain anything you have questions about. Whether about shifters, or how to heal from what has been done to you. Her partner, Dale, is human but knows all about shifters as he not only lives with one, but his daughter, Tina, is mated to Conner, Jake's youngest son. You would be safe in their home, have the freedom to come and go as you please, and have any questions you may think of answered immediately."

When Rachel stepped away, Xander didn't try to stop her. He knew there was nothing he could say or do that would have her being comfortable coming back to his house, and Dale and Jennifer's place was only a few streets away from him.

"Both myself and Kit also live in Rosebery."

Rachel rolled her eyes at him. "Of course you do. Kit had told me you didn't permanently live in Hobart. I think Kit told me but I can't remember what she said—how far away is Rosebery from here?"

Unable to resist, he went to her and tugged her against his body. She was stressed and he was compelled to comfort her. It's what mates did for one another.

"It's about a four and half hour drive. Far enough that you won't be accidentally running into anyone from Hobart on a regular basis."

For a glorious few minutes she softened against him and just as he thought she was going to stay there, she tensed and pulled away. Xander swallowed his sigh. One day he'd win her trust and her heart. Hopefully, it wouldn't take him too long.

"Okay. I'll agree to meet them, and only if I'm comfortable will I stay with them. Otherwise, I'll stay at a hotel until I can work out what to do."

"I know how badly you desire your freedom, Rachel, but do not be foolish with it. If you wish to stay in Tasmania, Rosebery is where you will fit in best. It's where a large leap is based and you will also find the acceptance and knowledge you seek there."

The longing in Rachel's gaze as Choden spoke once more cracked his heart wide open.

Chapter Nine

Wiping the sweat from her palms on her jeans, Rachel entered the Top Pub with Xander tight on her heels. The big white stone building was quaint in its old world charm on the exterior. It wasn't all that much different from Classic Convicts. Except for having one single apartment upstairs, they'd expanded and made it into a hotel with several rooms on the upper floor. Once inside, she was taken aback at all the updated furnishings. Someone had recently spent some serious money getting the place looking modern. It was immaculate, unlike Classic Convicts had been. Rachel chewed her bottom lip as Xander directed her through the room. She needed to stop comparing everything to that place. It was gone and all the horrible memories needed to die with it.

Of course that was easier said than done.

As they approached a table set for six, the four people already seated stopped talking and turned toward her. Kit was the only one she knew and before Rachel could say a word, the woman was up and pulling her into a tight hug.

"Damn, girl, it's so good to see you." Kit stood back a step and eyed her from head to toe. "How are you? How badly did that bastard hurt you?"

Tears pricked Rachel's eyes at the concern Kit was showing her. They barely knew each other and she was clearly distressed at her having been hurt.

"It wasn't pretty, but this man, Choden, came and visited me in the hospital. It turns out I'm like you, but it had been blocked somehow when I was a child. Choden released it and helped me to heal completely. So, I'm out of there and it's over."

Shock rippled over Kit's features before she shook her head with a grin.

"Should have guessed that a male as alpha as Xander was going to end up mated to a shifter. And you can't know how happy I am that you're out of that place and away from that bastard. Now, come meet the others."

With Xander chuckling behind her, Rachel allowed Kit to drag her closer to the table where the others stood waiting.

"Okay, this bloke is my mate, Jessie."

"Hi, Jessie, it's lovely to finally meet you in person."

He gently took her hand to firmly shake as he spoke. "I could say the same. Kit's told me some about you and your situation so I'm extremely happy to see that you've broken free from it."

Rachel's heart lurched that so many seemed to know about her troubles. Did the whole damn world know how big a fool she'd been? Blinking against her stinging eyes, she smiled weakly before she dropped Jessie's hand.

"Rachel?"

Suddenly all she could see was Xander. He'd turned her

to face him and now he stood before her with her face cupped between his palms. His skin was callused and so warm. Her cheeks tingled at his touch and she couldn't seem to tear her gaze away from his. He leaned down and her breath caught. She couldn't kiss this man. Not yet. She wasn't ready to go there with any man, let alone one as big and strong as this one. His lips landed against her forehead in a soft kiss that sent a flush of heat through her from head to toe.

"Relax, baby girl. They only know about you because I needed help working out how to get you free. You'll find no judgment here."

She squeezed her eyes shut against the rise of emotion that clogged her throat, then stepped back from him. He was simply too much. Definitely too good to be true.

"How about we all sit and order our lunch? We can chat over the meal and a few drinks."

Rachel swiped a thumb under each of her eyes to catch the moisture she hadn't been able to hold back, before turning to the woman who'd spoken. The older woman was smiling gently and it was almost more than Rachel could handle. She wanted to turn and run, get the hell away from all these people that were being nice to her. She didn't want pity from anyone. But before she could bolt, Xander rested a hand against her lower back and guided her to sit down.

"We boys will go order. Daily special okay?"

Feeling the need to be as low maintenance as possible she nodded. "Sure."

"You want anything to drink?"

"Um, just a lemonade, thanks."

She didn't want anything in her system to dull her senses. She still needed to work out whether she could trust the older couple, who she assumed were the ones Choden had suggested she live with.

"I believe Choden told you about me. I'm Jennifer and that's my partner, Dale." She nodded toward the three men standing at the bar waiting to order.

Rachel frowned. "You said 'partner' not 'mate'. Is there a difference?"

Jennifer smiled sadly. "My mate passed away years ago. We are given just one mate, but we can fall in love with more than one person. Dale and I went to school together and last year we reconnected and things kind of fell into place for us." She shrugged. "I'll always miss Ryan and my heart will never be whole again, but I love Dale and he's helping me move forward with life."

"What about Dale's mate?"

Jenny chuckled. "Dale is fully human. He was married, but has been divorced for a number of years. His daughter, Tina, is mated to Conner. Jake and Sophie's youngest son—"

"And she's going to be making me a proud grandpa in about three months' time. Hi, Rachel, I'm Dale."

The men all sat back down, Xander next to her. His masculine scent surrounded her, which both calmed her and frustrated the hell out of her. She wanted to stand on her own two feet for a while. She didn't want, or need, a man. Not after Rocco had all but destroyed her.

"So, Choden told us that you were needing somewhere to stay while you get yourself back on your feet."

Jennifer caught her off guard and she ended up inhaling a little of her drink.

"Ah, yeah." She coughed a couple times to clear her throat. "The fire destroyed everything. I don't even have my passport."

Jennifer leaned forward and patted her arm lightly. "Well, we have a spare room that you're more than welcome to, for however long you need it."

Rachel tensed. She'd only just met them, she wasn't ready to accept their offer!

"Um, that's a very kind offer—"

Jennifer lightly gripped her wrist. "No, don't respond now. I know you don't know us from a bar of soap at this point. Let's have a nice lunch and chat a while first. Then you can let us know what you want to do. Okay?"

Blowing a breath, Rachel relaxed enough to smile.

"That sounds lovely."

With that, they all started chatting again. Their meals were delivered and thankfully, the conversation as they ate stayed light. Rachel relaxed into her chair and picked at her meal. These people clearly knew each other well and spent time together often. What would it feel like to be a part of a group like this? To have friends who truly cared. She took in how Jennifer and Dale behaved. They showed no anger at all, in either their words or actions.

Rachel chewed on her lower lip. Was the risk of trusting this couple worth the potential of finding a place in the world where she fit? Jennifer could certainly answer any shifter questions she had. And she was a psychiatrist, so the woman may be able to help Rachel get her head back on straight. It would also give her a roof over her head so she could start looking for work and find an immigration lawyer to help her work out how to stay in Australia.

Licking her lips she took a deep breath.

"Jennifer? I think I'd like to see that spare room you have."

Xander stormed into the conference room at the Rosebery Firehouse. Rachel had agreed to go stay with Jennifer and Dale, but she'd continued to refuse him. After he'd taken her to their house, she'd told him she needed time to find herself before she could be with any man. He was her mate! Not just some random bloke that would tear her heart out. Nope. As her mate, he only wanted to help her heal. To show her that not all men were assholes and that he would never do anything to harm her.

"She'll come around, Xander. Just give her a little time. Take your pride out of the equation and logically think it through. After what Rocco did to her, it's only natural that she'd want to step back from relationships for a while and heal."

He spun on Kit. "I could help her heal! It's my damn job as her mate to make sure she's protected. How the fuck am I meant to do that when she won't let me near her? Lunch had gone so well. She didn't complain once about me sitting next to her, or any of the times I touched her."

"You couldn't see her face. And clearly, you were ignoring how her body tensed each time you brushed your hand against her arm or leg. She's not ready, Xander. I know you are. I know you want to claim her. But you can't, at least not yet."

Knowing she was right didn't help his mood. With a growl he spun away from her.

"Sean, any update from the hospital?"

He didn't need to say what about. The entire leap was waiting for news of how their Alpha was doing.

"Jake's still in a coma. It's not looking good. He should be healing by now."

Xander took a deep breath and released it slowly. If Jake were brain dead, he wouldn't be healing. Anything else, he'd have bounced back by now. He felt so fucking useless. His mate and his Alpha were both in trouble and there wasn't a damn thing he could do for either one. Well, there was one thing he could do that was useful. He could go clean house.

"Right. Well, sitting around here on our asses isn't going to help any. Boys, get all the information you have on the Triggers you found. We're going hunting. I want to head out in two hours. We'll be staying at least overnight in Hobart, probably longer, so repack your bags and be here ready to roll."

He didn't give anyone time to argue, as he turned and rushed from the room. He headed home, double checked his bags contained everything he'd need, then returned to the station to wait for the others.

Joel and Jordan were the first to return and when they entered the conference room, they wasted no time in spreading out their map of Hobart.

"We'd already marked all the locations we found. We were formulating a plan of attack when everything went to hell."

Xander planted his fists against the table and took in the map as the rest of the team filed into the room.

"Where had you planned on starting?"

"Well, Classic Convicts was always going to be our first stop but next on the list is this one. His name is Mick, and as far as we can tell is on the same level, if not higher, than Rocco. Never know our luck, we might find Rocco there." Joel pointed to a red spot two streets away from the bar as he spoke.

"Right. We'll start there. Who else have you got?"

Jordan stepped up and spread out a dozen head shots. "Here's the ones we've identified and located."

Joel took over and pointed out on the map where each of the bastards lived.

"I know it'll be late by the time we reach Hobart but I want to start tonight. It'll be easier to stay hidden from any innocent bystanders at night. I don't want to muck around with this operation. I want to clean house. Every Trigger we find dies. We'll go in with Kit, Jessie and me in human form, and Sean and the twins in leopard form. If we let the animals do the killing, they'll look like animal attacks. The authorities will write it off, and Trigger will hear of it and know not to mess with us again. We'll do this for Jake. For

Rachel. For Nick. For every one of us these bastards have ever hurt."

He held Sean's gaze. They all felt Nick's loss, but Sean had been the man's best friend.

"Damn right we will."

He nodded to the younger man. "Right. Everyone know what they need to do?" His team all nodded. "Let's move out then."

Sitting crossed legged on a bed that wasn't hers, Rachel's heart thundered in her chest. She couldn't put this off any longer. Choden had given her some facts, but only her parents could fill in the blanks. Until now, she hadn't had the ability to call them so she hadn't focused on it. But now she had a laptop in front of her, and Skype open and ready to go. All she had to do was hit call and she'd be patched through to her folks. Would they even answer her call? She tried to think of the last time they'd spoken. It had been months. They'd expressed their dislike for her choice in men, employment and where she lived. Basically her whole life. It had been such a pain to muck around finding an Internet Cafe, then getting her Skype to work, she'd stopped bothering. She couldn't see the point of going to all that effort just to listen to her parents insult her every life choice.

The little green light next to their names showed they were online. She had hers falsely displaying she was offline. She didn't want to deal with any incoming calls.

Rolling her shoulders and taking a deep breath, she

collected her courage and hit the call button. The sooner she did this, the sooner she'd have answers and she could move forward. Looking into her own eyes as the video feed rolled while the call rang had the knots in her stomach tighten. Tears pricked her eyes as it kept ringing. Would they really refuse her call?

A small ding and the screen altered to show the feed from her parents' webcam. Her mother's frowning face filled her screen and Rachel could do nothing to stem the tears that flowed down her cheeks. She may not have called them in a long time, but she loved them and the familiarity of her mum's face broke her control.

"Oh, darling. What's wrong? Why are you crying?"

Rachel sucked in a breath and tried to speak but she just sobbed as her mother called out to her father.

"Rachel? Sweetheart, tell us what's going on. We haven't heard from you in so long, we've been so worried."

Her father's face pushed in front of her mother's and Rachel held a finger up before she leaned over and grabbed the bottle of water from the bedside cupboard. She took a drink, allowing the cool liquid to ease her throat. Snapping a tissue from the box she dried her face, then focused back on the laptop.

"I'm okay. At least now I am. I've had an interesting couple of days. Learned some surprising things."

Her father rearranged the screen before he sat back with her mother. She could see both their faces now, and they both looked tense. She had so much inside wanting to break free, so many questions, but she had no idea where to start.

"Why did you do it?"

Her mother winced and her father tilted his head. "Do what?"

"Make it so I didn't know who I was. Surely you realized I would be found by my mate eventually."

Her frustration grew as her father's shoulders slumped and her mother covered her face with her palms, but stayed silent.

"There had to be a reason. You couldn't have been so cruel with no purpose."

Now she'd seen a little of how the leap here in Tasmania functioned, she wondered how different her life would have been if she'd grown up within a leap back in the UK. She'd at least know how to bloody shift forms. Choden had explained how, she'd seen Xander do it, but she was scared to try it herself. What if she couldn't? Or she got stuck as a leopard?

"We did it to protect you."

When her father didn't continue, she raised an eyebrow at him. "From what?"

"From the Alpha of the leap we were with. Alastair used to be a great leader, but when he lost his mate, he fell apart. The man he became after that wasn't very nice. Every fifteen years or so, he'd take a new lover. He'd force one of the young women in the leap to become his mistress after they shifted for the first time, until he tired of her. There were lots of fights from the true mates of those girls. Of course, he'd had them six years by the time their true mate's began dreaming of them. You were born soon after he took on a new girl." Her father paused to rub his eyes. "Even as a toddler, Alastair watched you with way too much interest. So, we quietly found a magic user to dampen your shifter abilities. Your mother, she's not a shifter, so when we told Alastair you were human, not shifter, he believed us. You were, of course, too young to be shifting, but even young shifters heal rapidly, have faster reflexes. That kind of thing. We told Alastair it wasn't fair to you to be raised among the leap when you wouldn't be able to do what all your friends could. He agreed and we left. Every now and then he sent someone to check in on us, and each time they witnessed how human you were and went back to report exactly what we wanted them to. By the time you left for Australia, he'd gotten over his fascination with you."

Her mind was reeling. She wondered if Choden knew about Alastair. He seemed like such a gentle soul, she couldn't imagine him being okay with one of his shifters behaving in such a manner. Rachel decided next time she saw the older monk, she would have a quiet word to him about it all.

"Okay, I get why you did it, but why didn't you tell me when I reached adulthood? No way would I have gone with this Alastair bloke."

Rachel winced as her mother broke down into huge sobs. Her father pulled her into his chest as he turned back to her to explain.

"An Alpha has powers normal shifters don't have. One

of those powers is the ability to lock down members of their leap. Sweetheart, you wouldn't have had a choice—or a chance."

Allowing her father time to console her mother, she reached once more for the bottle of water and took a long drink. Her brain whirled with all the information.

"Now, can you tell us else has happened? I can see the strain and lack of sleep in your face."

As quickly as she could, she recounted the fire, her escape, Jake being injured and Xander finding her.

"Your mate sounds like a good man. You're at his place now, I take it? Can we meet him?"

She shook her head. "He's not here. I'm not staying with him. I just got away from Rocco. I don't want, or need, a man in my life, Dad."

Her father glared at her hard enough to make her squirm even though he was half way around the world. "What?"

"Where are you if not with your mate? Who's taking care of you?"

She sat straighter as anger began to build. "I am perfectly capable of taking care of myself, Dad. Choden told me about an older couple who had a spare room, so I'm staying with them."

Shaking his head, her father mumbled something under his breath.

"You can't keep pushing him away, Rachel. You were predestined to be together. That means you were made to be together, to be the perfect complement to each other. His number one priority now he's found you, is to keep your safe, protected and cared for. Surely, you felt a connection with him? Why would you send him away? You're needlessly hurting him and yourself."

Her father looked so confused and her mother was still sniffling next to him. She hadn't mentioned Rocco's abuse in her earlier description. Some things parents didn't need to know. But she couldn't explain her actions without confessing what she'd suffered. With a huff, she scrubbed her face in her hands.

"I didn't want either of you to ever know. I'm not real proud of what I let happen."

"You can tell us anything, darling. We love you no matter."

Wetting her lips, she figured the quicker she got this out, the faster they could all move on from the subject.

"Rocco wasn't a nice guy. Turns out he's a Trigger, whatever the hell that is. Over the past eight months, he's gotten worse. He started getting physical with me a month or so ago. The day before the fire, he beat me—"

"He did what? Where is the bastard now?"

Her father's voice had gone ice cold and sent a shiver up her spine. She'd never seen this side of him.

"Um, I have no idea. Like I said earlier, Xander carried me out of the burning building while Jake took off after Rocco. Now he's missing and Jake's in a coma." She shrugged as guilt swamped her.

"I see what you're thinking, missy. Stop it. None of this is your fault. You didn't choose to be abused. This is all on Rocco's shoulders. Especially if he's a Trigger."

"No one has said who Trigger is. Do you know?"

His face set in grim lines as he took a deep breath.

"Trigger are enemies to all shifters. They hide behind a company facade of being a research facility but they're not. At least, that's not all they are. Mostly, we only see their gangs and operatives that spread like a vile disease across each continent, trying to find and destroy all shifters they locate."

She thought over what Rocco had said the last few times they'd spoken. She'd thought he was just rambling bullshit, but maybe not. She needed time to process everything she'd learned over this past week.

Telling her parents she'd call again soon, she signed off and shut down the laptop. She slipped off the mattress and stretched before she took device back to Jennifer. Thanking her, she asked to borrow a notebook and pen. Then she headed back to her room to write out what she could remember of what Rocco had said, along with everything Choden, Xander, Jennifer, and now her parents had told her. Things didn't make sense in her mind and she hoped by writing it all out she could process and make sense of at least some of it.

Chapter Ten

Once the team arrived at their Hobart house, none of them took long to dump their bags and be ready to go. The air around Kit buzzed with a mix of fury and excitement as they each prepared to leave for the first address. Sean had brought his huge van down. Being a shifter, he'd had the suspension reinforced to handle being loaded with leopards. As the three going in as animals hopped in the back to shift out of sight, Kit kept an eye on Xander. He was on edge and Kit worried he'd get hurt tonight. Physically he was ready to go fight, but Rachel's rejection had cut him deep. Kit was an expert at hiding her true emotions, so she could clearly see Xander was battling with his inner demons. Like her, he was dressed in all black and had a ski mask/balaclava rolled up to reveal his face. They didn't want to harm any innocent women or children, so they needed a way to keep their identities hidden if the need arose.

She sensed Jessie strolling up behind her. When he wrapped his arms around her waist, she sighed with a smile and leaned back against the warmth and strength of her mate.

"*Mi amor*, you're not planning to be reckless tonight are

you?"

She couldn't help but grin. The last time they'd gone
head to head with a bunch of Triggers, she'd been a little
overenthusiastic to get into it. She'd been like Xander was
tonight.

"No, babe. This time my focus will be watching
Xander's back. Not that I'd turn down the chance to knock
around a few Triggers, but Xander's not in his right mind.
He could easily make a decision he won't be able to
recover from if he's not careful. I plan to make sure that
doesn't happen."

Kit took a deep breath and closed her eyes as Jessie
rubbed his cheek against the top of her hair.

"Do you think we drove everyone crazy like Xander and
Rachel are now?"

A laugh bubbled up and escaped at the subject change.
"Are you serious? We were so much worse than them. You
literally ran for the hills and I turned into the bitch from
hell. I think the entire leap was ready to lock us in a room
together, until we learned to play nice."

His embrace tightened.

"I was a fool to run from you."

"You totally were, but lucky for you I love you so all is
forgiven."

She moved around to face her beautiful mate so she
could pull him down for a kiss. The moment their lips
touched, sparks flew. She'd never get enough of this man.
No matter how long they lived, it would never be enough.

"You don't go playing the hero either. I plan to grow

very old with you by my side the entire time. You understand?"

He pressed a quick kiss to the tip of her nose. "Yes, ma'am. Unless things go all to hell, I'll be in the van to keep it running for a quick getaway from each location. It's you and the boys that need to watch yourselves."

"You two lovebirds done?"

Xander's voice had a mix of frustration, impatience and a little humor as he called out to them.

"We're coming, keep your knickers on."

Jessie gave her one last squeeze before he headed to the driver's door. She climbed in the back, gave each of the three leopards a head rub, then sat down. They were all her leap brothers, and each one had been there to watch her back when she'd taken down her father only a few months ago. It was now time for her to watch theirs.

As the car rolled away, she took a deep calming breath, rolled her shoulders, wrists and ankles, and prepared herself for a night of fighting.

Jessie pulled up on the side street and Xander silently slipped from the vehicle. With his sensitive hearing, he hoped to pick up how many were in each home before they infiltrated. There was no one around, so he didn't bother rolling down the balaclava. He wasn't doing anything more than standing on the footpath for the moment, and didn't want to attract attention, which is what would happen if he strolled around looking like a bugler.

Taking a deep breath he calmed himself and focused on

the house on the other side of the fence.

"Dammit!"

Xander slammed his way back into the van. There was only a woman, who was talking on the phone, and what he guessed was a child sleeping. He could pick up the heartbeat and it didn't sound like an adult. That, and they knew Mick was married and had one child.

"Mick's not there, let's keep moving."

He'd known their luck wasn't good enough for them to find Rocco and Mick at the first house, but that hadn't stopped him from being hopeful. He was burning for a fight. Having his mate within his grasp, yet being unable to hold her, along with Jake not healing, had him close to an edge that was going to take some serious carnage to dull.

From everything they'd found out, since their raid in Rosebery a few months back, Rocco and Mick were the highest ranking Triggers in Tassie. Xander wouldn't stop until he had both of them taken out.

When Jessie pulled up next, it was to a house that clearly had a party going on in the back yard. This time Xander didn't get out, just wound the window down an inch or so and focused on the yard and house beyond.

"House is empty. And—"

He counted the different voices he could hear, but stopped when he heard the topic of their discussion.

"Interesting. There's at least seven in that yard, they're all male and all Triggers. They're discussing how they have no idea what they're meant to be doing now that Rocco and Mick have gone missing and Classic Convicts is no longer."

"It should be fairly easy to take them out. They're relaxed and I'd guess they've been drinking for a while already. We should be able to get in and out in no time. If Kit and I walk in from this side, we can distract them, while the boys come in over the back fence. Hopefully, we'll have them all taken down before they realize they're in trouble."

Xander nodded to Kit. Fighting was her arena. She'd been raised by a martial arts specialist before he kicked her out at fifteen. She could fight better than anyone he'd ever seen, but she was street smart too. Her mind was created for battle tactics and Xander had no issue taking her advice.

"Sounds good to me. And no one is surviving this round so we don't need to stress about keeping our faces hidden. It's a hell of a lot easier to fight when you've got full range of your vision."

They both stepped free of the van, checked no one was on the street, then opened the rear door to let the boys out. The three snow leopards quickly melted into the shadows as they prowled to the rear of the property. The homes around this one were all silent and dark, so Xander was confident they could do this with no witnesses.

"C'mon Kit. Let's get this done."

With a roll of her shoulders, she gave him a quick nod and they marched off toward the front of the house. Wanting to maintain an element of surprise for the moment, they slipped down the side of the house until they reached the rear yard. Seven men sat, beers in hand, around a fire pit.

"You boys know there's still a fire ban right? Fucking idiots. Middle of summer and you've lit a fire. No wonder we're so busy, huh Xander?"

Xander chuckled. Kit was a smartass. But she'd done the job. They currently had all the attention squarely on them.

"You're that big bastard who's been coming in and checking out the boss's woman. What the fuck do you want?"

Folding his arms over his chest he stared at the one who'd spoken.

"Guess Rocco doesn't share information with those under him, because when I saw him yesterday, he knew exactly who and what I was."

Kit pulled her balaclava off and tucked it into the back pocket of her jeans, shaking out her fiery red curls. They were pretty bloody distinctive. "Maybe you're not well known enough, brother. I know after I took out Gab word got around about me."

"Fuck! You're freaks!"

There was a clatter as beer bottles were dropped and the men scrambled to their feet, apparently just realizing the danger they were in.

"Yeah, we're the freaks." Kit shook her head. "It's you fools that run around killing innocent shifters. All we do is protect, and occasionally serve justice. You lot come after us and kill whoever you can get your hands on. Well, tonight we're turning the tables."

Too late, the men turned to see what Kit was looking at behind them. Sean, Joel and Jordan stalked from the shadows toward them rumbling low in their throats. Xander braced himself as Kit did the same beside him when three of the seven turned to run from the approaching leopards. Idiots thought he and Kit were less dangerous.

Xander stayed where he was, blocking the side exit of the yard, while Kit rushed forward to place a hard fast punch to the first guy's throat. The bastard went down coughing and gagging as he tried to breathe. A second man swore and faced off against Kit in a fighter's stance. Nothing pissed Kit off more than an incompetent opponent, and this fool was going to feel her full wrath.

The third man stayed clear of Kit and rounded on him, like maybe Xander hadn't noticed him.

"You're not leaving here. Not after all you've done."

The man lunged at him with a growl and Xander traded kicks and punches with the obviously trained Trigger for a few minutes, before Xander managed to land a solid kick to his chest that sent him reeling back. Straight into the path of Sean. The huge snow leopard reared up behind the bastard and in one smooth movement, wrapped his paws around his torso, digging his claws in deep. As the man began to scream out in pain, Sean sunk his teeth into the back of his neck and snapped his spine. Along with opening up arteries that made one hell of a mess of the ground around them.

He turned from the soon-to-be-dead man to take in the carnage around them. All seven Triggers were mauled and dead. The boys had been sure to make enough scratch marks on the bodies to make it obvious a rather large animal had done the damage.

"Right. Let's get out of here."

As Jessie drove from the street, Xander pulled the map out along with the head shots they had of the men. He picked out two he was certain had been back in the yard, and crossed their places off the map.

"This one, and I reckon that one..." Kit paused to hold the photo up to the boys. Sean nodded his head.

Xander crossed those two off the map. Then held up each photo to the leopards so they could nod or shake their heads. It would have been easier for them to shift back, but the blue glow from their shifts would attract attention. Someone would soon discover the massacre they'd just left behind as a couple of those men had screamed before they'd died. Xander was certain someone would have dialed emergency. They needed to get away from here as quickly and quietly as they could so they could go deal with the Triggers who were left before word spread. Police scanners could be a bitch.

Dominic stared at his father, still not believing what had happened. His dad was Alpha of the leap. The man was indestructible. But he lay before him in a coma, a machine breathing for him.

He sighed and pulled his mate in a little closer to his body. Adele had taken leave to stay with him, his brother, his pregnant mate, Tina and their mother. Kelly was staying with a friend from school, so she could keep up with her studying. She still had so much to catch up on.

They all spent their days crowded in Jake's hospital room, often with Choden by their side, as they waited for a miracle. At night after they got kicked out, they all went back to a hotel, but Dominic hadn't slept. In the thirty-six hours since his father had been injured, he'd not healed at all. Despite them all praying and hoping for a miracle, Dominic knew deep down it wasn't going to happen. There wasn't much a shifter couldn't heal from. But there were a few things, nasty options like a broken neck, being brain-dead, or having a failing heart.

He jerked when his phone started ringing. He pulled it from his pocket, intending to end the call but when he saw who was calling he knew he couldn't. He gave Adele a quick kiss on the top of her head.

"I've got to take this. Back in a minute."

He slipped out into the hallway as he answered the call.

"Hey Alex, this is a really bad time. Can whatever it is wait?"

"Sorry, Dominic. I heard about your Dad. He's not improving then?"

Alex was a detective who lived in Rosebery. He knew about shifters and helped them out when he could, just as the shifters helped him. Alex would often call in their help with missing kids and tourists. The leopards knew the Cradle Mountain National Park better than anyone and could find those lost in no time. But Dominic doubted this call was anything to do with the park.

"No, he's still in a coma. What's this about?"

"I hate to bother you, but with your dad out, that makes you Alpha right?"

Dominic cringed. He always knew he'd be next in line but he'd never wanted to take the role because his dad was gone.

"Yeah." He paused to clear his throat. His voice was so rough. "I guess so."

"I've just seen a couple reports come through the system. Seems there were several large animal attacks last night in Hobart. We've got fourteen dead. Don't suppose you know of any of yours that are in town?"

Dominic cursed under his breath. It had to be Xander and his team, but he wouldn't throw them under the bus. He needed to be careful. Alex was an ally, but he wasn't one of them.

"I haven't spoken to anyone in nearly two days so I'm not sure who's where. I can look into it."

Alex's voice grew soft. "Dominic, I've read the reports. I've seen the photos of Rachel. Your dad told me about the Trigger issue after what happened to Nick. I'm guessing these bodies the police have are Triggers and justice has been delivered. When you find who's done this, get them to contact me. And don't worry, I'm not going to lock anyone up. These cases have been listed as animal attacks and besides the local boys now carrying tranq guns in their vehicles, nothing much will come from it. Well, aside from the media kicking up a stink. What I'm worried about is your guys becoming vigilantes. It never ends well with untrained civilians doing this kind of thing. I've got some ideas that could help whoever it is, if they really want to get some justice."

Dominic held his breath as Alex finished speaking. Then with a frown he held the phone tighter.

"What are you saying exactly? That you want to make a team of us cops?"

"Not exactly, and I really don't want to discuss it any more on the phone. Just find whoever did this, tell them to stop until they see me. You come with them if you want. I'm on your side, Dominic. And I think I have a way to make what you all want to do easier."

"I'll see what I can do and get back to you."

He ended the call and slipped back into his dad's room. He didn't know what to do and his dad wasn't available for advice. *Fuck.*

"That was Alex. Seems Xander and his team got a little carried away last night. I need to go deal with them."

His mum looked him in the eye. "You don't sound like that's all he said. What is it? I'm not your father, but I've learned a thing or two over the years. Talk to us, son."

He glanced around at Conner, Tina, Adele and his mum. Choden hadn't come in yet today, unfortunately. Dominic was sure the older shifter would know what to do.

"Fourteen men were killed in animal attacks last night. Alex isn't going to arrest anyone over it, but he basically said he knew it was us that had done the killings. Apparently Dad told him about Trigger after Nick, and Alex wants to chat with whoever is doing these justice-killings. He told me he has an idea to help make it more legit somehow. I don't know what to do."

Adele wrapped her arms around him and hugged him close. He closed his eyes and absorbed his mate's love, needing a moment to just be still with her.

"In all the years we've known Alex, he's never gone back on his word. He's never once shared our secret, and has always helped when he could. I believe you can trust him with this. However, I'd make sure Xander knows not to verbally admit to any killings. No sense in putting Alex in that kind of situation. He is a police detective and has sworn to do his job. I don't think his conscience would allow him to look the other way if someone told him outright they'd killed men."

Raising his head from where he'd rested it against Adele's, he looked at his mother, processing what she said.

"That's what I was thinking too. I mean, as long as no one admits to anything, there's no harm in going to hear him out, is there?"

She nodded at him with a faint smile. "Now you need to go deal with Xander and his team. If the attacks continue past one night, they'll be a massive hunt launched for any animal big enough to cause this kind of damage. It will cause all sorts of issues for us and the local wildlife for a long time."

"I know, Mum. I don't want to leave, but I have to. They're still in Hobart as far as I know, so I shouldn't be gone too long."

He gave his mate a deep kiss, losing himself in her taste

and scent for a minute before he reluctantly pulled free of her and strode out the door. He couldn't look at his dad before he left. Seeing the man so pale and still was ripping his insides to shreds. *Please, give us a miracle.* He wanted his dad back more than anything. He wasn't ready to say goodbye to the man who'd raised him and guided him through every stage of his life.

Freshly showered, Xander stood at the large dining room table as he studied all the information they had. They'd managed to take out fourteen Triggers last night, but Rocco and Mick weren't anywhere to be found. Where could the bastards be?

Joel and Jordan sat with their laptops open and were constantly tapping away and cursing, as they clearly weren't finding anything useful either. Xander frowned as he looked over the map with the location of all the homes. Surely they had some other meeting place other than Classic Convicts? The houses weren't in any kind of pattern, they weren't even in the one suburb. There was nothing about the locations that gave him a clue to where they might have a hideout.

A solid knock at the door had him jerking toward it.

"I'll get it."

Kit was out the room before Xander could respond. He straightened and moved to follow her. Not many knew they were here, so he was curious who it was. He wasn't worried it was a Trigger. If it was, Kit would handle them with speed and efficiency. He reached the front hallway to see Kit wrapping her arms around Dominic. The poor bloke looked like hell. Then again, if it was his father in the hospital in a coma, he imagined he'd look just as bad. The whole leap was feeling the pain of Jake being down, but not to the extent his direct family were.

"Hey, man. Any change?"

Dominic shook his head as he pulled away from Kit. "No change. Is everyone here?"

"Sure, we're all in the dining room. Come on through. Want a drink?"

"Coffee would be great, if you've got a pot brewing."

Jessie rose from his seat as they entered the room. "Of course we do. I'll grab you a cup."

Dominic slowly strolled around the table, glancing at the map and at the laptop screens as he went. Once Jessie returned, Dominic thanked him for his coffee and took a mouthful before he cleared his throat. Xander frowned at him. Whatever the man had come to say was big.

"I got a call from Alex a little while ago. Seems Hobart had some trouble last night with big animals attacking men."

Xander tensed and crossed his arms. "You knew what we would do. The goal all along has been to take out this Trigger cell. We just upped the timeframe."

"I know, Xander. But fourteen in one night, when you don't clean up after yourselves isn't the way to do it. C'mon, man. You know better than this! Look, Alex said the deaths are being ruled as animal attacks but it can't continue. You and your team need to pack up and go home.

Alex told me to get you to contact him. He swears he's not going to try to nail you on these murders, but that doesn't mean you should flaunt the fact either. Apparently he has some way to help us. It seems Dad told him about Trigger after Nick, and he wants to help us. I'd recommend meeting with him before you head off on your next trip. I know you're all keen to get moving, especially Kit. You've waited a long time to see your mum again and I'm sorry to delay that down longer, but if Alex has some way to make what you're doing legal, it'll really help long term. Alex invited me to come with you guys when you do meet, so just let me know when and where and I'll do my best to get there."

Xander closed his eyes a moment, trying to calm his voice. They were so close to ending this Trigger cell, he could feel it.

"Rocco and Mick are still out there. This isn't over yet."

Dominic moved to stand in front of him, the man's inner alpha flashing in his eyes.

"I wasn't asking, Xander. I'm ordering you as Alpha to stop the bloodshed. Rocco is going down for what he did to Rachel, and what he did to my dad. He will get caught, and the police with deal with the bastard. I don't know who Mick is, but leaving one alive just means that we can be sure word will travel higher up the food chain at Trigger. Your role here is done. Your team has completed its task and now it's time to go the fuck home." Dominic softened his stance and gripped Xander's shoulder firmly. "I've got enough on my plate right now, I don't need to be fending off anxious cops and hunters searching for large animals. We'll end up with shifters being killed in the park. I understand you want revenge and justice served. Trust me, I get it. I do. But is it worth the cost? The last thing any of us need are vigilantes taking over the national park, taking pot shots at us and the local wildlife. Think this shit through. I know Dad trained you on how to deal with bodies if you killed Triggers. And it sure as hell wasn't to leave them where they lay in the middle of a suburban backyard."

All the anger drained from Xander's body as he felt Dominic's words hit him like a punch to the gut. He'd been feeling hurt from Rachel's rejection, guilty over Jake's injuries and he'd been impulsive when he should have been patient. Dominic was right to be here kicking his ass. Xander pulled from Dominic's touch.

"I'm sorry to have laid more shit on you. We'll all head to bed for a few hours, then later this afternoon we'll head home."

Without glancing at any of his team he walked out and headed to his room. He couldn't get his emotions under wraps and he didn't want anyone to witness his meltdown.

Chapter Eleven

Two days later Xander sat at his parents' dinner table and tried to ignore their stares. He shoved the food around the plate but couldn't muster up the focus to eat anything. He wanted his mate. *Needed* her. Xander had left her his number and told her to call him whenever she wanted, for anything at all.

But she hadn't called. Not once.

His heart ached with not being near her. He could only guess how confused and overwhelmed she felt after learning about being a shifter and that her parents had done something to hide her abilities. He hadn't called her because he was being a coward. He hadn't managed to catch Rocco. He was her protector, he should be out there slaying her dragons—but he'd failed. And now he'd been ordered to stop trying.

The house phone ringing caught his attention and he watched as his father left the room to answer it.

"What's on your mind, sweetheart? You know you can talk to me about anything."

He shrugged. He didn't want to go into things with anyone. He was struggling enough without analyzing it all.

"I miss her. That's all."

She reached over and wrapped her hand around his forearm gently. "Of course you do. She's your mate and you're meant to be together. It'll all work out, you'll—"

She stopped talking and tightened her grip on him so suddenly, Xander knew something was wrong before he glanced to the doorway to see his very pale looking father gripping the doorframe tightly.

"Jake. He. Hell, he's gone. They made the decision to turn off life support and he passed away about an hour ago."

His mother gasped and ran to her mate. Numbly, Xander watched them embrace as tears flowed from them both. Xander's mind whirled. Jake was gone. His Alpha, the man who'd always been there for him, had trained him to fight fires, had given him the job of running this first anti-Trigger team, was gone.

Because of him.

If only he hadn't left him alone in that fire. If they'd just waited for the full crew to get there before they went in. Why didn't they just wait for back-up?

With his eyes stinging, he pushed back from the table and turned to leave. He didn't listen as his parents called out to him. He had one destination in mind and he wasn't going to stop until he had Rachel in his arms. Blindly, he got in his car and started it up. When he looked out the windscreen everything was blurry. What the fuck? He wiped at his eyes with the heels of his palms and they came away wet. Dammit, he was crying. He shook his head. It didn't matter. Rachel could see him cry. Aside from his father, no one had impacted his life more than Jake. It was only natural for him to shed a few tears at the loss. He wouldn't be human if he didn't.

Shoving the car in gear, he made short work of the three blocks to get the Jennifer and Dale's place. He skidded up to the curb and bolted from the vehicle, barely pausing long enough to hit lock on his key fob before he was pounding on the door. A red-eyed Jennifer opened the door tentatively, until she saw it was him. Before Xander knew what was going on, he was wrapped in her arms for a brief, but strong, hug.

"Go to her, she needs you. She's blaming herself and nothing I say will get through to her." She pulled back and held his arms so he couldn't run off on her. "You're doing the same thing aren't you? This is not your fault, any more that it is hers. Rocco is the one who is at fault. We might not know exactly what happened, but something did for Jake to get thrown like he was. You hear me, Xander? Not. Your. Fault. Blaming yourself isn't going to help anyone."

Xander winced as Jennifer saw straight through him. She made a good psychiatrist because she could read emotions in people.

"I hear you. But it's hard to not blame myself. There's a lot of 'if onlys' that I could have changed."

"There always are. But even if you had done every single one of those 'if onlys', there's no way to say we wouldn't still have come to the same outcome. Ultimately, we'll never know, so there's no point in beating yourself up over it. Grieve the loss, sure. But don't take the blame for it."

She released him with a gentle nudge toward the rear of the house where Rachel's room was. As he strode down the hallway, anger that Rocco was still out there free had him clenching his fists. He wished he could tell Rachel he was gone and would never bother her again. As it was he had no idea what he was going to say to his mate. He just knew he needed to hold her close.

He hoped she'd let him. His fingers itched with his need to caress her. The door to her room was closed and he rested a palm on it as he wrapped the other hand around the doorknob. He could hear her weeping. She was trying to keep quiet and he doubted anyone other than him would have heard her, but he heard her loud and clear and it broke his heart. He slowly pushed the door open, stepped in and closed it behind him before he turned toward her.

She lay on the bed, curled into a ball with her face pressed into the pillow. The sight of her looking so fragile and broken hit him like a freight train and he stumbled over to her.

"Baby girl..."

Lost in her grief and guilt, Rachel didn't realize she was no longer alone until Xander scooped her up off the mattress. As he rolled her against his chest, she looked up and noticed the tears on his face. Shock stilled her for a moment. This huge tough man was crying? She'd often heard that saying that real men didn't cry, and she couldn't recall ever seeing any man cry before now. Xander's tears and rawness reached her soul and broke her open. She couldn't stand that she'd caused this man so much pain.

"I'm so sorry."

As she spoke, she flung her arms around his neck and buried her face against the warm skin of his throat. His strong arms tightened around her as he pressed a kiss to the top of her head. She gasped and pulled her face back when he jolted her, to see he'd stepped up on the bed. Within moments, he sat and settled against the headboard with her in his lap.

She wriggled a little to get more comfortable but stilled when Xander's large palm caught her cheek.

"Baby girl, none of this is your fault. Why are you sorry?"

Chewing on her lower lip, she held his gaze. Could she tell him the truth? Would he turn her in? She couldn't risk it. With him surrounding her, she felt safe and protected. She didn't want to risk losing it when she so desperately needed it.

"If it weren't for me, you and Jake wouldn't have been at Classic Convicts."

"No. That's where you're wrong. If it wasn't for Rocco, we wouldn't have been there. If you weren't being abused, we wouldn't have had to rescue you. This is on Rocco's shoulders. Not yours, and not mine. I tried to get him for you, but I failed. We caught so many, but we missed the one that counted most. I'm sorry. I failed you."

She couldn't ague that everything that had happened was on Rocco's shoulders. She never would have lit that damn fire if he hadn't locked her in like he had.

"What do you mean? You tried to get him? Where have you been these last few days?"

His gaze moved over her face as he started stroking her hair. She shivered when he ran a fingertip down her nose and over her lips.

"You wouldn't have me. Jake was in hospital. I had fury to burn off and tracking down Triggers seemed like a good place to aim it."

As his constant gentle touches calmed her, she loosened her grip on his neck, moving her hand so she could run her fingers over his hard chest. Every muscle was defined and huge. He had so much strength, yet he always showed her nothing but exquisite care.

"I've heard that term several times now. What is a Trigger?"

Of course, her parents had explained a little, but she got the feeling Xander knew more about them than what she'd been told so far. His chest expanded against her as he took a deep breath.

"Trigger is a research company. Publicly, they research and create pharmaceuticals. But their real purpose is to wipe out shifters. The have people all over the world who watch for signs of shifter activity. When they detect it, they pull in a team and do their best to wipe out any leap they find. They're bastards who don't care about anyone but themselves. They kill men, women, children—it doesn't matter."

She frowned up at him. "And you think Rocco is a

Trigger?"

"Rocco is definitely Trigger. The tattoo on his neck? The one that looks halfway between a cat's eye and a rifle trigger. That's their logo. The reason we came in that first time was to investigate him. We're done being their victims and Jake put together a team to go after them. We're turning the tables. Kit, Jessie, Joel, Jordan, Sean and I. That's why we went to Hobart—to find and shut down the Trigger cell there before they found us."

She closed her eyes against visions of Xander running in a rampage across Hobart.

"I saw the paper yesterday. Fourteen dead in one night to animal attacks."

She whispered the words, not daring to ask him outright if he was responsible. Could she accept someone so violent?

"While I technically didn't deliver any killing blows, I was there for each one. I'm the leader of our team, baby girl. It's my job to keep my team safe as we take out threats to all shifters. Look at me." He paused until she forced her eyes open to look up at him. "I'm not like Rocco. I will never raise a hand or paw against an innocent. Did you read that report? No women or children were harmed. We only took out those men who we knew were Trigger. No one else. And I'm so sorry but we couldn't find Rocco. He's disappeared."

"I don't want to even think about that man ever again. Tell me, what would you do if you found a shifter abusing innocents?"

He stiffened and frowned down at her.

"I would never stand by while an innocent suffered, no matter if they were human, shifter or animal. Choden explained how we were created, and it was for the purpose of protection. That hasn't changed, it's ingrained in shifters to want to protect those around them. Especially those they love."

She watching him as she thought over what he said. She traced her fingers over his bulging bicep. He certainly had the strength to do whatever he wanted to her, or just about anyone. Yet, he hadn't. He could have snatched her from the bar at any time. He certainly didn't have to facilitate her meeting Jennifer and Dale so she could move in with them. He really hadn't done anything to warrant her pushing him away, and she was tired. Too worn out to remember why she shouldn't give in to exploring the connection she felt with this man. But she did want a few more answers first.

"Not all shifters." He tilted his head in question and she lifted her hand to trace the edge of his jaw as she continued to speak. Now she'd started touching him, she couldn't seem to stop. "I spoke to my parents the other day and they told me why they had my abilities hidden. It was due to their Alpha taking lovers by force. According to my parents, he'd lost his mate, so every fifteen years or so he'd take one of the young females as his after her first shift—regardless of her will, or that of her destined mate. They'd seen him take notice of me even as a toddler, so they used the fact my mother is human to fool him into believing that I, too, was human by having my abilities blocked with magic."

Fire flashed in Xander's gaze. "We need to tell Choden about him. He can't know it's going on, because if he did, he would have intervened. Did your parents tell you his name?"

She nodded. "Alastair. No idea on his last name, but I'm sure Dad would be happy to tell Choden whatever he wants to know. So, does that happen often? Shifters hurting others?"

Xander's fingers trailed down her neck and stroked over her shoulder.

"I've never heard of it, but I guess like any species there are going to be good and bad. Choden has, well, spooky powers. He seems to always know when things are about to go bad and appears to assist. I'm not sure why he hasn't dealt with Alastair, he must have somehow not known. But I think that's why we don't have many issues among shifters, Choden intervenes as soon as he can and puts a stop to problems." He shrugged one shoulder. "It may be one of the jobs our team gets given to take care of. Jake had explained to me that he had bigger plans for us than just taking out Triggers."

His voice trailed off as his fingers kept up their exploring. Her own hands were far from idle. She'd mapped out every inch of the man's upper back, shoulders, chest and arms. A gasp tore from her and her back arched when he brushed down the outside of her breast. It had been the barest of touches, yet it burned her all the way to her core.

Xander had his mate in his arms. He could scent her arousal as he caressed her gently. He couldn't stop touching her now he'd started. All his anger, guilt and grief washed away as he filled his lungs with her delicious scent and felt her fingers glide over his upper body. He leaned down to press a kiss to her temple, leaving a trail of them all the way down to her lips. He hesitated for a moment, with his lips hovering over hers, silently asking for permission as he held his breath.

She rose to press her mouth against his and his whole world narrowed down to just her. Moving his hands to frame her face, he deepened the kiss. A groan tore from his throat when she parted her lips on a gasp and he got his first taste of her mouth. He could kiss this woman forever and be happy. She tasted so sweet. His whole body tensed when her soft hands trailed down his torso and slipped under his shirt. He broke the kiss as he hissed out a breath. Her touch seared him, it was so hot.

Wanting more contact with her, he gripped the back of his shirt, between his shoulder blades, and pulled it up over his head. A grin spread over his face as Rachel's eyes stayed glued to the flesh he'd revealed. Her fingers lifted to his tattooed biceps and chest where she started tracing the designs. She shifted to straddle his lap and when she settled in, he gripped her hips. A moan left him, when she pressed herself against his rock-hard erection, making it throb.

Her eyes flew wide as though she hadn't been fully aware of what she'd been doing. Pressing her palms to his pecs, she wriggled back a fraction. "Sorry."

He tightened his grip on her hips and pulled her back close to him.

"I like you close, pressed against me. Although, I wouldn't complain if I could see a little more of you."

He ran his gaze down her front before lifting to look into her eyes once more. A sweet blush had bloomed over her cheeks.

"I'm not as perfect as you. I have soft bits."

He tried not to laugh. He really did, but a small chuckle escaped, which earned him a glare and a pout.

"Baby girl, you are meant to have soft bits. I think you're beautiful with clothes on, and I'm sure I'm going to like what's underneath just as much, if not more. Please, won't you show me? Just a little."

As much as he'd love to see her naked, he knew now wasn't the time or place for that. He just wanted to feel her skin against his when he kissed her again. When she pulled her lower lip in between her teeth, he began rubbing his thumbs over the flesh just above her jeans in small circles in an attempt to relax her. He wasn't going to push her beyond what she was comfortable with. Just as he was going to go let it go, she wrapped her fists in the bottom of her shirt and peeled it off. Xander's mouth went dry at the simple black satin that was revealed. It was so Rachel. Simple, but classy and sexy as hell. He moved his palms up to touch more of her midriff. She was toned and clearly kept herself fit. Her tummy had the sweetest little bump that had him instantly wanting it swelling larger with his cub. She complained about her soft bits, but they were his favorite parts.

"You are gorgeous."

In one smooth move, he ran his palms up her back to pull her against him. Her breasts pressed against his chest as he took her mouth in another scorchingly hot kiss. She swiveled her hips against his and the pressure against his throbbing erection was nearly enough to have him messing his jeans.

Panting, he pulled away from her mouth and kissed his way across her jaw. He loved how her skin tasted.

"Come home with me, baby girl. I promise I'll take care of you. I don't want to stop touching you, but I know we can't go much further here. I don't want Jennifer and Dale listening in when I take you the first time."

She arched into him as he nibbled on the edge of her ear for a moment then with a gasp, she flung herself off his lap. Shocked, he frowned as she scrambled in a panic to get away from him. He scrubbed both palms over his face, trying to clear his mind. Each new rejection from her was another deep slice into his already bleeding heart. With his mind now clear of lust, the full force of his grief, guilt and shame filled him. Could he do nothing right? He'd led the team so well Jake had died. He'd protected his mate so well she was scared of him. Hell, he hadn't even been able to take out Rocco for her. Now he was trying to seduce her when she was upset and scared.

Ignoring the sting behind his eyes, he slowly moved to the edge of the mattress. He needed to leave Rachel alone.

She'd made herself clear that she wasn't ready for a relationship. He'd stupidly hoped because they were mates he could get her to change her mind, but clearly that wasn't going to happen. He rose to his feet, then froze. Where to go? He guessed his house was the most logical, but he didn't want to be alone, especially in the place where he'd wanted to share a life with Rachel.

Fuck it all, but he needed his mate. Even if he knew it was impossible. He hung his head as he put his hands on his hips, and tried to think of something. Anything to say to Rachel, whose gaze he could feel burning into his back.

Chapter Twelve

What had she been thinking? Rachel had cost a man his life, a man Xander clearly adored. Oh, he'd tried to tell her it wasn't her fault but he didn't know what she'd done. From the moment Xander started kissing and touching her, her brain had turned to mush and she'd forgotten all the reasons she shouldn't give in to the attraction bubbling between then. She pulled her shirt back on, trying to ignore the way the skin above her hip bones still tingled from his caresses.

Sucking in a deep breath she turned to face him. She expected him to be furious with her. Rocco never would have allowed her to stop things mid-way like that, but him reminding her of where they were was like throwing a bucket of cold water over her libido. Jennifer and Dale would kick her out if they knew what she'd done. She wasn't sure what Xander would do.

What she found broke her heart. He wasn't mad, at least she didn't think he was. He stood on the opposite side of the bed, facing the door. His shoulders were slumped and his head hung down. He looked defeated. And so achingly sad she teared up.

Frowning, she rubbed her chest, her heart actually

hurting. She had a suddenly overwhelming need to soothe and comfort him. It had been her that caused him this pain, she needed to fix it. Or at least try to. She slowly, quietly padded over toward him. He lifted his head as she rounded the corner of the bed. She stumbled at the stark pain in his dark eyes.

"Oh, Xander. I'm sorry. I'm so bloody sorry."

He crumpled down to sit on the edge of the mattress before he scrubbed his face in his palms.

"I can't just walk away from you, Rachel. I know that's what you want, and I wish I could give it to you —but I can't. You're my mate. I know I've failed you, and you have every right to be angry with me. I should have gone searching for you sooner. Maybe if I'd gone after you when I first dreamed of you, I'd have found you before Rocco did. I could have saved you all of this and you wouldn't be frightened of me now."

He was breaking her heart with each word he said. She had to confess her crime to him. She couldn't stand seeing him so cut up over her when he should be washing his hands of the whole thing. Including her.

She stepped between his knees and he wrapped his arms around her waist to pull her in further. She was short enough, his face was level with her breasts and he nuzzled his face against them. Unable to resist, she leaned down and pressed a kiss to the smooth skin on the top of his head as tears tracked down her cheeks.

"You'll soon change your mind about leaving me once you know what I did. All of you will."

He tried to lift his face but she held him to her, pressing her wet cheek against his warm skin.

"Nothing will ever make me turn you out. You are mine, my perfect other half."

A sob wrenched from her. "And I ruined it all. I didn't mean to. I just wanted to be free. I'd rung Kit and she couldn't come, she was working. So I." She paused to take a breath. "I lit a fire so she would come. I swear I didn't mean for it to get so big. It was meant to stay in his office. But I didn't think about all the alcohol down there." Her voice cracked, her shame was now out in the open. She tried to push away from him, unable to bear seeing his expression change into hatred toward her. "*Let me go.*"

Her whole body shook as she cried in great heaves but she still struggled to get free while avoiding looking at his face. Without releasing her, he stood and on instinct she cringed down as she covered her face.

"Fuck me."

His curse was low and said under his breath a moment before she found herself on her back on the mattress with his large frame caging her in. Shock had her forgetting she didn't want to see his expression, and she blinked her eyes clear to look up at him. Now he was truly furious. Would she ever stop making the men around her mad?

"I'm sorry, Xander. I never meant for anyone to get hurt! I promise. I just wanted to get free."

His gaze softened and he leaned down to press a kiss to her forehead. Every time he kissed her there, she melted. It was like there was some kind of switch there that only

Xander knew how to flip.

"Rachel, I'm not mad you lit the fire. Yeah, it was stupid and dangerous, but you were in a shitty situation and got desperate. No one is going to argue that with you. I'm mad that you're scared of me. I will never hurt you, baby girl. I'd rather die than see you suffer in any way. Can't you see that? Why didn't you call me that morning? You had my number."

Lifting her trembling hands she caught his face between her palms. The heat from his skin soaked into her and she took a few deep breaths.

"You know some of what Rocco did to me. How can I not be wary of men now? I can see that you care about me—"

"I love you, Rachel. I always will. We're mates, baby girl. Born to complete each other. This isn't some high school crush, or a rebound fling. This is forever. I know that's scary, but look inside yourself. You feel the connection to me deep down, just like I do. You know I'm safe. And I'm sure I don't know all that bastard did to you, but I'll make sure none of it ever happens to you again."

He turned his face and kissed her palm gently. He was melting her resolve to be an island. He knew what she'd done, and he hadn't turned her out. She thought over what her parents had said about mates. They hadn't questioned that Xander was hers at all, just accepted that their daughter would settle down here with him. Maybe she needed to give him a chance. He was beautiful, and he clearly cared for her... she could easily fall for this man. That's what was really scaring her. She'd never felt for Rocco what she already felt for Xander.

"So you want me to move in with you?"

His whole face softened and a smile tugged at his mouth.

"More than anything. I want you in my arms always. I need to know you're protected and safe. It's been driving me crazy, not being able to lay eyes on you for days at a time. Please, baby girl, say you'll come stay with me?"

Still holding his face in her palms, she guided him down to her until their lips met. He took over the kiss within seconds, demanding entry and possessing her body and soul with just the touch of his lips against hers.

As she relaxed into the bed she had to admit, just to herself, that she'd already fallen hard for this man.

"What the hell do you think you're doing?"

Rocco glanced up from the table in Cherry's kitchen at Mick, who'd just barged in.

"I'm eating just at the moment. Do you have a problem with that?"

"Don't be a bastard. You know what I mean. Your bar is in ashes, and those freaks took out fourteen of our men last weekend. We should be well away from here until we can get enough back up to take out this leap. Yet here you are, shacked up with one of your strippers."

He shook his head at the other man as he swallowed.

"You can go running off to the higher ups if you like, but you might as well have laid down and let those animals gut you, because if we go back with nothing to show but losses, we'll be the next ones on the chopping block. No, I learned something in that fire. Something I intend to use to barter with the higher ups for my life. But without proof it's useless. So, I'm going to stay here, make the most of what's available, and keep an eye on them all for a few days. When an opportunity arrives, I intend to capture at least one of them using what I've learned. Then I'll call in the higher ups."

Mick huffed as he pulled out a seat and dropped into it. "It seems like you have it all planned out. What did you call me in for? Doesn't sound like you're going to share what you discovered with me."

"Not until I know if you're in or out. If you want to take your wife and kid and vanish, be my guest. If you want to stay with Trigger, well, we'll talk."

He wasn't going to force the man to stay and fight. Mick had always made it clear his family came first. And hell, Rocco kinda liked the idea of claiming full responsibility for working out a new weak spot in the shifters. However, he knew he'd have more luck at succeeding with Mick's help.

"You know full well, if I were going to nick off I'd have been in the wind days ago. So, c'mon. What's the big secret?"

"You see the paper today?"

Rocco grinned at Mick's frown. He tossed the newspaper over to land in front of him.

"One of the firefighters died? What the fuck?"

"Nah, that's just the spin they're putting on it. Does the name look familiar? Jake White would be the name I was given for the local Alpha down here. He and that big bald bloke came after me that day. I was dealing with Rachel for lighting the fucking fire when the pair came barging in. I threw Rachel down the stairs and ran, Jake followed me. All I had on me was that new Taser Trigger sent all of us, so I used it on him. But it caught him at the precise moment he was between man and beast. You know, when they're surrounded by that blue bubble thing. The shock jolted him out of the shift and he went flying, still in human form. He crashed through the floor and from what I've read, he couldn't move. The firefighters that pulled him out saw him come through the ceiling near them and land heavily. His eyes were open but he didn't appear to be able to hear them calling out to him. A beam came down on his head and he didn't even attempt to halt it."

Mick rubbed his jaw. "That's a serious weak spot, but yeah, we need to test it more before we go reporting on it. Have you got a plan?"

"All the shifters that were in Hobart are gone, so I went for a drive yesterday and can confirm they're all holed up in Rosebery. I'm going to give them a day to two then I'm going to head out there and wait for a chance to grab Rachel. She's our best bet. I doubt it will take long for that bloke to mate her, then he'll do whatever we want for her safe return. If they truly are completely unresponsive after shocked, they'll be easy to cuff and send off."

Mick frowned at him. "Why wait?"

"If we go in now, they're running high on emotion. They're unpredictable and will be more likely to take risks. Nope. It's better to give them a few days. Hopefully, they'll think we've run off and not even be on guard. This will work, especially with two of us."

"We just need to keep our phones turned off until then, huh?"

Rocco chuckled. "Yeah, the higher ups are not going to be happy about losing that many in one night, that's a given."

He stood to go put his dish in the sink. He couldn't wait to see Rachel again. Maybe once he had her new man all trussed up and helpless, he'd take her again.

Once more for old time's sake.

Before he shipped the pair of them off to the higher ups for them to do whatever the hell they did with shifters and their mates.

Despite all the shit that had happened today, Xander grinned as he followed Rachel up the path to his front door. He had her bag. The small backpack contained all his mate owned since the fire had taken everything else. Xander had slipped Jennifer some cash to take Rachel shopping—he'd guessed she would refuse to accept his money if he'd tried to give it directly to her. He wasn't sure what she'd do if she ever found out he had funded the small shopping trip. He'd given Jennifer enough to buy a lot more than she had, but Rachel had refused to buy more that she needed to survive, as she didn't want to take too much from her new friend. Jennifer had also told him she'd kept their house clean and cooked for them to pay them back. His mate was an independent little thing.

As soon as he was certain she'd let him, he'd take her shopping to get all she needed. But for the moment, he was simply content to finally have his mate living in his home and sleeping in his bed. And she would be. Xander didn't care if Rachel thought she was going to go to bed alone tonight. If he had his way, she never would again. His fingers twitched with wanting to touch her as he reached around her to unlock the door. He brushed his chest against her back, and relished the way she shivered as she, for a brief moment, leaned into him. With a grin, he pushed the door open.

"Welcome home."

She stiffened. "This is your home, Xander, not mine."

"We're mates, Rachel. What's mine is yours, so this is now your home too. Go on in and have a look around. I'm afraid I'm not much of a decorator. You can change whatever you want."

She glanced over her shoulder at him with a frown before she silently shook her head and strode into the house. She was going to keep making him work for her. Good thing he liked a challenge. He left her to wander around while he went to put her bag in his, no, *their* room. With a smile on his face and his heart feeling lighter than it had in months, he went to find his girl.

He found her looking out the back sliding door, motionless with her arms folded over her chest.

"Do all shifters have yards that open into bushland?"

She looked so fragile standing there, his instincts screamed at him to comfort her. So he moved to stand behind her, and wrapped his arms around her waist as he inhaled against her hair. The tension left her as she leaned against him with a soft sigh, which had him in turn relaxing, as he kept her close.

"We prefer to. It means we can shift and go for a run whenever we feel the need. Of course, most of us prefer to head out deep into the national park where there's no people to worry about. I can take you out there whenever you like."

He wanted to ask if she'd shifted yet, but didn't want to risk her pulling away from him so he stayed silent and began to move his hands. Slowly, he slipped beneath her shirt and stroked the smooth silky flesh just above her pants. His fingers tingled and he shuddered as the sensation ran through his whole body. She arched against him before she shifted her hand back around his waist. He sucked in his breath when her fingertips slipped beneath the waistband of his jeans, to give her more room to touch him.

He lowered his head and pressed kisses down the side of her face until he nuzzled her neck. When she moved her free hand to glide up to cup the back of his head, holding him to her, he slid his palms up until he cupped both her breasts. He gently kneaded the fleshy mounds, loving how she writhed against him. She wriggled her butt against his groin and his dick throbbed with need.

She released him and started to turn to face him. He

gripped her hips and spun her the rest of the way, before he pushed her against the glass of the rear door and took possession of her mouth. Images of how beautiful she looked half naked flashed behind his eyes. He didn't get long enough to enjoy her earlier, but now they had hours. Days to learn each other in the privacy of their home. He ran his hands down to cup her bottom, and lifted her against him. She wrapped her arms and legs around him and pressed small kisses and nips to his neck and jaw.

"Baby girl, you are playing with fire."

She laughed until he ground her core against his rock-hard erection, then she moaned and clutched him tighter as he walked across the house with her.

"What are you doing to me?"

He stood her next to their bed and before she knew what he was doing, he had her clothes off. He pulled his own shirt free then kissed her again. He managed to keep the contact as he toed off his shoes and stripped out of his jeans and boxers.

"Nothing yet. But I'm going to make love to you, baby girl. I'm going to make you feel so good, you'll never want to leave me."

He pulled back from her mouth, ripped the sheets down, then lifted her against him. He paused a moment to enjoy the feel of all her smooth, silky skin sliding against his own, before he moved to lay her on the bed, following her down. She tensed when he lowered himself over her, giving her some of his weight.

"I'd never hurt you, baby girl, especially not like this.

Will you let me love you? If you're not ready, that's okay.
I'll just hold you and we'll do nothing but sleep all night
long."

He hoped she didn't say no. He would honor her choice,
but it would leave him hurting for a damn long time. His
body was wired and ready to roll with claiming his mate.
He knew that wouldn't happen tonight, no way was she
ready to accept his mark and to bond with him forever. But
he desperately hoped she was ready to let him inside her
body.

Tears pricked her eyes at Xander's words. The man was
actually asking for her permission. Rocco had always just
taken what he wanted. Her feelings or readiness never
mattered. She caressed her fingers over his face before she
cupped it between her palms. The moment she touched
him, he stilled completely and locked his gaze with hers.
There was so much heat she swore she could feel herself
grow warm from it.

"I'm going to freeze up on you. I don't mean to, but
things keep reminding me of other times and my mind
locks up on me. But I know you wouldn't hurt me."

At least she hoped like hell he wouldn't. She already felt
more for him than she ever had for any of her previous
lovers. If he decided to hurt her like Rocco had, she wasn't
sure she could survive it. That was the main reason she'd
tried to keep her distance, but she couldn't do it. The
connection between them was too strong and after hearing
from Choden and her parents about what being mates

meant, and seeing how Kit and Jessie and the other mated pairs she'd seen in the leap interact she was finished trying to keep her distance. Her heart ached to have that kind of relationship with a man. And not just any man, her heart only wanted Xander.

"We'll work through it, Rachel. I'll give you countless good memories to replace those shitty ones, and before you know it, there will be no room in your mind for him at all. It will all be filled with you and me, and all our good times."

The sincerity on his face and the emotion in his voice had tears pooling out of her eyes and tracking down to land in her ears. He leaned down and kissed away the moisture, making her cry harder. She moved her hands to the back of his head and pulled him down to her shoulder as she buried her face against his neck. She didn't try to break away when he rolled them so she was on top of him and he had his strong arms wrapped around her like steel bands. The security and safety she felt when wrapped up by him was just what she needed. She nuzzled against his bare chest and tried to stop the flow of tears. She hated that she was so broken she couldn't just give in to this man. He was so beautiful and gentle. He was her gentle giant. Oh, she knew he could be vicious and deadly when he needed to be. She had no doubt he played a vital role in the deaths of those fourteen men in Hobart. But with her, he'd never even shown a flash of temper.

Eventually she ran out of tears and with her body flush up against his much larger, harder one, she let go and slipped into sleep. She was so damn tired.

When she woke she was curled against Xander's side. He was on his back and she had her head on his shoulder while her arm was draped across his wide chest. His arm was against her back, with his palm cupping her bare bottom, keeping her tucked in close against him. Moonlight streamed through the open curtains to reveal he was sound asleep. She tilted her face to glance down his body. During the night the covers had fallen off both of them and Xander's long, muscular body was revealed in all its glory. Damn the man was big all over. His hard pecs rose and fell with each breath he took. She barely resisted the urge to trace her fingers over the indents marking his abdomen into a six-pack any male model would envy. Her gaze kept going, past his hips to where her leg was over his thigh. His dick was large, even now when it was soft. How big would he be erect? Her core tightened at the thought of taking him inside her. Would he even fit? A soft tremor ran through her as she wondered if it would hurt.

She sucked in a breath and heat began to coil in her lower abdomen when his erection twitched and began to stiffen before her eyes.

"Like what you see, baby girl?"

Xander's sleep-roughened voice had Rachel's cheeks heating with embarrassment at being caught ogling him as he'd slept. She pulled her hand back to press against his ribs, as she attempted to shuffle away, but he tightened the arm behind her, keeping her pressed against him. His other hand came up and he stroked fingers over her hot cheek.

"Don't be embarrassed. I liked the way you were

looking at me."

A chuckle bubbled up from her throat. "Ah, yeah. I can see you woke up happy."

She moved her thigh to lightly brush against his erection, earning herself a moan from him.

"I have my naked mate in my arms. Of course I woke up happy."

She wasn't ready to talk about mates and forevers, so she did what she knew would distract him. She reached her hand down and gripped his hard length in a tight grip, then began to stroke him. For a moment he stilled, his whole body tensing. Then with a growl he rolled them so he was on top and took her mouth with such fierceness her mind emptied of all her worries. He left her mouth to trail kisses down her throat as she panted and arched beneath him. She grabbed fists full of the sheet when he suckled her right nipple while he kneaded the flesh he couldn't get in his mouth. Sparks jolted her system, landing between her thighs.

"Xander!"

He lifted up and moved until he was lying between her legs. A tremor ran through her when he lowered and she could feel the hard hot length of him against her mound. She whimpered when he flexed his hips and slid up and down a few times against her. He had her wet and ready for him and he'd barely touched her! No man had ever had this effect on her.

Xander didn't give her time to ponder that thought for long. He shuffled down her body, kissing and nipping as he went until he had his head between her thighs. She propped herself up on her elbows to see what he was going to do to her next. The look on his face had her heart rate kicking up several notches. He was completely focused on her as he ran his big, work-roughened palms up her thighs, spreading them wider. He slowly lowered his mouth toward her core and a moment before he made contact, he looked up and caught her gaze. Fire burned in his eyes and she couldn't look away as he licked up between her folds for the first time. Her body tensed and he moaned against her.

"You taste so good. I need more."

With a gasp her arms gave out and she fell against the mattress when he returned to her core and began lapping and thrusting his tongue inside her. Panting, she lowered a hand to hold his head to her as she moved her hips to grind against his tongue. It felt so bloody good. She was going to lose control soon, she couldn't risk it. She'd be too vulnerable in that moment. It was something she'd never given any man, or herself.

Using both hands she pushed at his shoulders as she jerked her hips back from his mouth.

"I need you inside me, Xander. Now. Don't make me wait."

Chapter Thirteen

Licking his lips, Xander prowled up his mate's perfect body. He could have stayed between her thighs all damn night and still not gotten enough of her. She tasted better than anything he'd ever eaten or drunk in his life. All sweet and musk mixed together. He nuzzled against her breasts and nipped at her nipples before laving them with his tongue. She squirmed beneath him and moaned his name.

He reached over to pull out the drawer on his bedside cupboard to grab a condom. Good thing he was an optimist and had bought a packet to have on hand a few weeks ago. As fast as he could, he grabbed one free and slid the latex over his throbbing dick. He could hardly believe he was about to make love to his mate for the first time. So many nights he'd dreamed of this moment, but it was so much sweeter in reality. He wanted to tell her he loved her, but could tell from her expression she'd bolt if he did.

"I've waited so long for this, baby girl. I can't wait to be inside you."

She reached up, wrapped her arms around his neck and pulled him down to her. He went willingly, delving into her mouth when she opened under his lips. He tugged on her lower lip before breaking the kiss to turn enough so he could watch as he lined his erection up with her slick core. How he wished he didn't need the condom. He'd love to feel her, flesh on flesh. *One day.* He comforted himself that one day soon, there'd be no barriers between them.

Her wet heat engulfed the head and he blew out a breath to keep control. Fuck. He was going to come in moments if he didn't get himself under wraps. Not taking his eyes from where they joined, he flexed his hips and slid in deep. Rachel arched against him as he fully entered her and he couldn't resist the nipple that was now thrust up against him. He palmed her breast and sucked on the tight bud as he started a slow, strong rhythm with his hips. She was so hot and soft, he knew he'd never want to leave her body. He lifted his face to look at her. Her eyes were squeezed shut and her mouth was open as she panted. Her fingers gripped his shoulders tightly as he continued to rock into her.

"You are so beautiful."

Her eyes flicked open and she smiled at him. He stilled a moment, leaned in and took her mouth. He wished she'd agreed to be his mate. That this bout of love making would end with him claiming her for all time. She moved beneath him, putting her feet on the mattress and swiveling her hips against his. He grinned as he left her mouth.

"Sorry, love. I stopped moving."

He leaned back to kneel between her thighs, and cupping her hips in his palms, he began thrusting deep inside his mate as a faster rate. He was so close to coming—he'd known this first time he wouldn't last long, but he wanted her to come too. Even if he couldn't claim her, he wanted to experience climaxing with his mate. He moved one hand to begin teasing her clit as he continued to thrust into her. Her internal muscles clamped down on him and she screamed. That was all it took—and with a roar, he came, filling the damn condom while wishing it were her womb that was accepting his seed.

Purring, he nuzzled his face into her neck as he came down from the heavens. It took a moment for his brain to fire up and alert him to the fact his right hand was still fully human. When mates climaxed together, the male's right hand sprouted his leopard claws so he could mark her. He rolled to the side and held up his hand, flexing it to be sure it wasn't just taking a minute to happen. He frowned as his nails remained the same.

"What's wrong? What did I do?"

Her scared voice shook him free from his thoughts and he realized he'd clenched his fist. How could she think he'd hurt her? Damn Rocco for all he'd done to this beautiful woman. He cupped her face in his palm gently, then took her mouth in a slow and soft kiss.

"You were perfect, I didn't want to ever stop. Unfortunately, I couldn't hold off any longer. I'm sorry. I thought you'd climaxed but you didn't, did you? I've never done this before, baby girl. I have no idea what to do to help you. Tell me what you need me to do for you to get there?"

He was kicking his own ass, hard. His first time with his mate and he finished before her! How could he have not noticed? Although, he remembered her clenching down on him, and she cried out. Had she faked one? Why would she do that? Her face paled before she licked her lips.

"I don't know. I've never—you know. So I don't know what I'd need you to do."

Shock had him jerking back from her before he could stop the movement. In a burst of speed she rolled away from him and bolted to the en suite bathroom. Stunned, he lay there watching the shut door. He knew she wasn't a virgin. She'd been with Rocco for longer than the eight months they'd been in Tassie. How, in all that time, could the man not have given her an orgasm? A small part of him rejoiced that there was something he would be the first to give her, but his anger at her abuse easily overrode it.

With a sigh, he got up and headed to the main bathroom to quickly clean up. Once Rachel was showered and dressed, he was going to sit down with her and try to sort this mess out. He didn't want her avoiding him because of what happened between them just now.

Dominic stood staring out of the front window of his parents' home. He was aware of his remaining family in the room with him, knew his mate was by his side. Her worry and the grief pouring off her in waves strong enough he felt them through their bond, but he couldn't really connect to any of it. He was numb, body, mind and soul. His father was gone. The man who'd raised him, shown him how to be a real man. He'd taught him how to ride a bike, how to shift forms. Hell, he'd even taught him how to successfully hide a dead body as part of his Alpha training.

Fuck. He swiped his palms over his wet eyes. How was he meant to go on without him? He wasn't ready. The room going silent had him blinking his eyes clear and turning to see what had happened now. Choden stood in the center of the room, patiently waiting for Dominic to face him.

"Dominic, it is time for you to rise to Alpha."

He shook his head and winced as his tears flowed once again. "No. It's not. I can't. Not now."

"I know you are grieving. We all are, and will be for quite some time, but that does not change the fact the leap needs an Alpha. The position cannot be left empty."

Adele wrapped her arms around his waist as he drew her in close to him, her love and support strengthening him.

"*Mon amour*, you can do this. For the leap and for your father. He would want you to take his place."

He squeezed his eyes shut and shuddered against his mate.

"I know he wanted me to take over from him, but he was meant to be here to guide me as I did it. Dammit, he should have lived for at least another forty years!"

His voice cracked and he heard his mother's muffled sob. The sound cut him deep, like a bucket of cold water being thrown at him. He woke the hell up. He buried his face in Adele's hair, inhaling her scent deep into his lungs. He was being childish, pining for his dad while the whole leap suffered. Choden was right, of course. He needed to grow the fuck up, man up, and take the position that he'd been groomed to take. He decided in that moment he would not be the cause of any more of his mother's tears. He needed to make his parents proud, not ashamed as he wallowed in his grief and ignored his responsibilities.

With a deep breath he stood with his spine straight, and held Choden's gaze.

"I'm sorry for my initial reaction, I meant no disrespect. I am, of course, ready when you are to rise to take the position of Alpha of our leap."

Choden bowed slightly. "You will not be alone in this, Dominic. Any time you need help or advice, the Council is there for you and I am always available to help however I can. I will be staying here for some time while you adjust to your new role."

His heart ached with the loss of his father, but he looked around the room at his mother, brother, his heavily pregnant sister-in-law, and his adopted daughter, Kelly, who clung to his mother, her face buried in the older woman's shoulder. He blinked back the fresh round of tears and returned to look at Choden.

"What needs to happen to make it official?"

"The actual process is simple. I say a Tibetan blessing and bestow the Alpha powers on you. Normally it is done as part of a celebration with the past Alpha stepping down to allow the younger to take over. It is your choice on how you wish to proceed, whether you want it in front of the whole leap or a private ceremony."

He turned to his mother, he didn't want to disrespect her or his Dad's memory so wasn't sure which way was the right way to go. "Mum? What do you want do?"

Sophie smiled weakly, as she stroked Kelly's dark curls.

"The leap has suffered enough. I think a celebration would be lovely. We can celebrate your father's life at the same time. He would have preferred it that way, rather than a funeral where we all continue to cry for him."

He nodded as Choden began to speak. "We will incorporate a celebration of Jake's life with the ceremony for Dominic rising to Alpha. I do not want to rush things, but we need to have this happen soon. This leap here in Rosebery is strong and close-knit. Left with no clear leadership it will begin to crumble at the edges. I know how hard it is to lead when your heart and soul are grieving, but you must step forward and do so. Jake was your father, and you will never stop grieving for him, but the pain will get easier to live with."

A glance to his mother showed him she was at the edge of holding it together. Keeping Adele close, he moved to where he could wrap an arm around her and Kelly. Connor and Tina joined them and they just stood there embracing each other as they struggled to control their emotions. There were family, and Dominic knew their love for each other would get them all through this.

Somehow.

Chapter Fourteen

Rachel stood beneath the hot spray and cried. Bloody hell, she was so broken she couldn't allow herself to climax with her lover. She hated the look of hurt that had filled Xander's dark gaze. Reaching for the soap she began scrubbing her body, inhaling the woodsy scent of the soap that made her heart ache even more, as it was what Xander smelled of.

"I'm so stupid! How could I think this was going to end well?"

Tears continued to flow as she washed herself. Xander had left small red love bites over her chest. She touched the largest one. He'd marked her, but not like Rocco. Xander had marked her with passion, not anger. She huffed out a breath before she held it as she put her face under the spray. How had he known? None of her previous lovers had ever picked up on the fact she faked her orgasms. She'd honestly never had one. Never had a lover who cared whether she did or not. Clearly, somehow Xander had picked up on the fact she hadn't reached her peak and he was hurting because he came while she didn't. *Such a gentleman.*

The man confused her so much. He was huge and fierce,

but with her he was gentle and protective and so damn caring. She couldn't trust it. He was too perfect. And anything that good, couldn't be true. Could it?

After she washed her hair and did everything she could in the bathroom, she looked at the door and chewed her lower lip. She couldn't hide in here forever. She needed to go face the music with Xander. She'd wrapped the large blue towel around her already, so with a deep breath for courage she slowly opened the door to an empty bedroom. Tears pricked her eyes. Had he left her? Did he want her gone now?

Spying her bag by the dresser, she quickly got dressed and went to find if she was alone in the house. Opening the bedroom door, she was greeted with the smells and sounds of cooking. Relief flooded through her system that he hadn't abandoned her. As quietly as she could, she crept down the hallway toward the kitchen. She slipped into the room and watched the play of muscles in Xander's bare back and arms as he flipped something in front of him. He shifted around doing things she couldn't see for a few minutes until he spun and strode over to her with a look of determination on his face. Before she could think to run away, he had her trapped against the wall. He lowered his face and pressed small kisses down the side of her face until with a sigh, she relaxed against the plaster behind her. Turning her face to expose her neck to him, she shivered when, with a purr, he kissed his way down her throat.

A gasp left her when he slipped his hands under her butt and lifted her against him. Instinctively she wrapped her arms and legs around him.

"What are you doing?"

"I'm going to feed my mate, then we're going to have a nice long talk about some things."

She stayed silent as he grabbed a plate filled with a huge omelet from the counter, then moved to sit at the table. He maneuvered her so she sat on his lap sideways. She was so much smaller than his large body that sitting this way had their faces level. Wrapping one arm around her waist to keep her secure, he reached forward with the other to grab a fork and fill it with food. He brought the small mouthful of omelet up to her mouth, raising an eyebrow when she didn't immediately open.

"I can feed myself, you know."

"I'm well aware you can take care of yourself, however, I want to do it this time. Humor me? C'mon, open wide, before I start with the airplane noises."

She laughed and leaned in to take the food from him. She could imagine him feeding a child, making all the silly noises to get the little one to eat.

"I feel enough like a child without you making the fork into a plane or train."

His hand moved from her waist to slip under her shirt and up her spine. He proceeded to trail his fingers lightly over her skin, making her shudder against him.

"You look like a beautiful woman being taken care of by her mate. Nothing childlike at all."

She didn't hesitate to open for the next forkful that he raised to her. With his gaze on her, she felt cherished and protected. And his back rub had her relaxing completely. After she ate another few bites, he took a mouthful for himself and she ran a finger over his shoulder.

"Do all your tattoos mean something?"

He nodded as he swallowed. "They're mostly Tibetan symbols. Some for protection, others for courage. The artist has put a few curly bits between them all to make them flow together, but the bulk of them are all meaningful."

She dutifully ate the next mouthful, then ran her hand over his left pec.

"No tattoos on your chest?"

He grinned at her as he ate the last mouthful.

"That space is reserved for your mark, baby girl."

She frowned at him. "My mark?"

"Let's go sit on the couch. It's more comfortable."

She looped her arms around his neck as he rose, and he took her weight with no effort as he moved to his lounge. She tried to scoot off his lap but he held her in place.

"Please stay here. I like holding you and having your hands on me." He paused to take a few deep breaths. She got the impression he was trying to find the right words to say.

"Just say whatever it is."

"To complete the mating, a shifter couple have sex and climax together. The male's right hand will sprout his leopard's claws. Traditionally, the male takes the female from behind so when his claws sprout he uses them to scratch her here," he stroked his fingers over her shirt, just above her hip bone. "The female then spouts claws on her right hand, she turns and swipes them down over the male's chest." He took her palm and pressed it over his heart. "Here. It's magic based. I'm told it doesn't hurt at all. What is left afterward is four wide scratches that reveal our leopard spots. To the human eye it'll look like a tattoo. To any shifter who sees it, they know you're mated and not available."

She kept her palm against his chest, the strong beat of his heart resounding through her whole body.

"That's how you knew. Did you think we might not be mates?"

He shook his head firmly. "Never. I've been dreaming of you for years. I felt the connection between us when we met, the sparks that flew when we touched. No way are we not mates. Maybe if I had more experience I would have picked up on it sooner..."

She jerked her head up raising her gaze from his chest to his dark eyes. Was he really saying what she thought he was?

"That's the second time you've said something like that. How much experience do you have?"

His expression softened as he lifted his hand to stroke her face.

"I've always known I had one true mate out there waiting for me. Why the hell would I waste time with any other woman? No one could have ever lived up to you, so why risk getting another woman's hopes up?"

"You were a virgin?" She ran her gaze over his body

from head to toe. "I'm struggling to believe how a man as good looking as you could still be a virgin at, how old are you?"

"I'm thirty-one, and yeah, that's what I'm saying. There's more to life that how we look on the outside." He shrugged. "I'm sure I could have found a willing woman or two if I'd wanted to, but I had no desire. No woman has stirred my body or heart until I first saw you."

Shock had her speechless. He'd waited for her. Then it hit her. All the men she'd been with and her face heated. She hadn't been a hussy or anything, but she'd had a few lovers before Rocco. She winced.

"I'm sorry I didn't stay pure for you."

He stopped her from saying anything more with a kiss.

"You didn't know I was out there waiting for you, Rachel. I'm not going to hold anything from your past against you. I'm just glad you're here with me now."

As much as he loved that she now knew he'd been saving himself for her and only her, he hated that she was now beating herself up for not having done the same.

"I don't know how we're going to work this out. Are you even sure you want me? I'm—bloody hell—I'm broken alright? Especially when it comes to sex. My head is all over the place. I've never enjoyed it and I learned pretty early on that if I fake it, the guy gets off faster, then it's all done and we can cuddle."

His heart broke at her rush of words. She'd been offering her lovers sex to get the affection she craved.

Xander vowed she'd never feel that way again. He'd shower her with affection all day, every day. And he'd show her that sex could be wonderful, a soul shattering experience like he'd had with her. Guilt still ate at him that she hadn't felt that way about their first time together, like he did.

"I wish your parents hadn't hidden what you were from you. If only they'd explained, you'd have known that no one can love you like your true mate. Did you enjoy what I did to your earlier? Or did you fake all your reactions?"

He'd tasted her cream, seen how wet she was. He might not have had sex before this morning, but he'd made sure he knew his way around a woman's body. He'd wanted to be prepared for when he did find his mate. He knew she couldn't fake getting so hot for him that her body grew slick. However, he wanted to see if she'd try to hide it.

She squirmed on his lap trying to escape but he didn't let her. He knew she'd run like a rabbit if he gave her half a chance. They needed to have this conversation.

"You do know I can't make my body get wet on demand, don't you?"

Her cheeks grew redder and as cute as it was, he could sense she needed a break from his questions. Before he could say anything more a loud, solid knock at the door echoed through the house. He pulled Rachel in for a kiss. He took possession of her mouth, only backing off after she moaned for him.

"Yeah, I know. And I'm glad I can get you all hot and bothered. We'll finish this discussion some other time, baby girl. There's no rush—we've got the rest of our lives together."

He didn't want to push her so hard she ran, but at the same time he wanted her to be fully aware he was playing for keeps with her. Without giving her time to respond, he stood with her and leaving her in the lounge room, went to answer the door. He wasn't surprised when she followed a few steps behind him. He smiled as she hid around the corner so whoever was at the door couldn't see her.

A quick peek through the window next to the door before he swung it wide, had his mood taking a nosedive.

"Hey, Alex. What can I help you with?"

"Hi, Xander. I'm told Rachel Bell is staying with you. Is that correct?"

He cocked his head as he took in the man's stance. Was he on the clock or not? This didn't feel like a friendly visit from the cop, but he didn't have his cuffs out either.

"She's my mate, Alex. Where else would she be?"

A ripple of shock passed over the man's features. "You claimed her already? I was sure she was going to hold you off after what she's been through."

He folded his arms over his chest. "I don't need to have completed the mating to know who she is to me. What's this about?"

"Can I come in? I need to speak with Rachel. I'm not going to arrest her, so relax, big guy."

Taking a deep breath, he moved back and ushered the man in. He led him to the kitchen and called out to Rachel. He knew she was close, but wasn't entirely sure where she was currently hiding. She slipped into the room looking like a frightened rabbit. He snagged her arm and tugged her over to him, then sat down with her on his lap at the table.

"Right, Alex. Let us have it."

He could feel the tension building in his mate and knew she wanted to run from them both.

"In the remains of Classic Convicts we found a safe. The boys were quite impressed it remained intact after having all that rubble land on it. I believe Joe mentioned something about calling the company to see if they want it for advertising how indestructible the things are." Alex chuckled a little, but stopped when neither Xander nor Rachel joined in. "Okay. So, since Rocco has gone missing under suspicious circumstances, we were able to acquire a warrant to break it open. Turns out there were a few things in there with your name on them."

Rachel slumped against his chest and he began a soothing caress of her back with his palm. "He didn't put illegal stuff in my name did he? Because I was just the bar manager, I didn't know about all this other crap until after the fire."

Alex opened the case he'd brought with him and pulled out a pale yellow folder. He turned it around and slid it over the table to sit in front of Rachel.

"There were plenty of documents that the boys are going over in order to work out exactly what Rocco was up to, but these items are yours clean and clear. Did you realize he had your passport?"

Rachel stilled—even her breath stopped for a moment

before she shook her head and reached for the folder. She flipped the thing open and Xander watched as she fingered through her passport and other paperwork that looked like stuff to do with her immigration.

Emotions mixed and coiled inside Rachel. She was furious that Rocco had taken her passport and hidden it. Even if she'd managed to get out of the apartment the day of the fire, she wouldn't have been able to fly home or do much of anything without all these documents. The up side was, now she had them all safe and sound as Rocco was a paranoid bastard and had a top of the line fire-proof safe.

"I thought my passport was in my handbag which was lost in the fire." In a rush she brushed her fingers over her eyes. "I can't believe he'd take it and hide it like that, but I'm so glad I don't have to try to organize a new one along with all my other visa stuff. Thank you."

Alex reached over to give her hand a squeeze and Xander tensed beneath her.

"The cause of the fire is still being investigated. Looks like it started down in the lower level. All the alcohol down there had it burning pretty hot so it could take a while for the investigators to pin it down exactly, if they ever do. I know in your statement you said you were on upper apartment level when you noticed the smoke so I'm not going to hassle you for details about it."

Her throat closed up as a sob tore free. Guilt tore at her heart. She'd cost a good man his life, all because she wanted to be free. Should she tell this detective she lit the fire? She'd be arrested but didn't she deserve to pay for her crime? Before she could confess to anything, Alex was pulling another folder from his case.

"I had a friend of mine do some digging for me. One of those documents in that folder is your resume. It states you're a qualified chef. Is that correct?"

She frowned over at the detective, forgetting all about confessing to him. "Yes, that's right. I just finished my apprenticeship when I decided to come to Australia to explore. Why are you asking me about it?"

"I understand you were engaged to Rocco and a spousal visa was being processed for you. I take it you have ended your relationship with Rocco?"

"Um, hell yeah. If I never see that man again, it'll be too soon."

Alex smiled gently at her. "I thought that would be the case. I have some paperwork here for you to look over. There's a list of skilled occupations that the Immigration Department is actively looking for foreigners to fill. Chef is on that list. If you can find an employer to take you on before we lodge the paperwork, together with the recommendations from myself and other officers, I'm sure we'll get you a permanent Visa to stay here." He cleared his throat. "If that's what you want. If you want to go back to the UK, you are free to travel whenever you want."

Xander growled and held her closer to him. She absently patted his arm as Alex covered his mouth to hide what was obviously a laugh.

"I can really stay? It'll be that easy?"

"Well, it all takes time, but yes, I'm quite sure with your skills we can get you a Visa to stay independently."

"You could just marry me, and get that spousal thing."

Alex relaxed back into the seat shaking his head. "Sorry, that wouldn't be a good move. Rachel had one in the system already. To cancel one spousal visa only to reapply with a different spouse straight away would be frowned upon and it's highly likely to get rejected. And this way, you both know that Rachel is here with you because she wants to be, not because she feels trapped. I suspect Rachel, here, has had enough of being trapped."

She smiled at Alex before looking back at all the documents before her. She gathered them all up and slipped off Xander's lap.

"I need some time to think about all of this. Alone. Thank you so much for all you've done, Detective. I was really worried about how I could stay in Australia long term."

He smiled at her kindly. "No problem. And please, call me Alex."

She left the room to Xander offering him a coffee and made her way to the bedroom, where she sat with her legs crossed in the center of the bed and spread out all the information about the Skilled Worker Visa so she could start reading.

As much as she could feel how strong the connection to Xander was, and knew he intended for her to stay with him long term, the ability to stay in Australia on her own merits would be wonderful and give her a sense of freedom she'd been missing for so long. Excitement bubbled in her veins the more she read. This was really possible. A grin broke across her face when she recalled her trip to Top Pub earlier in the week. There had been a 'Help Wanted' sign taped to the bar. They were looking for a chef and bar staff. Since she was skilled in both areas, and was living locally, she hoped they'd consider her for the job.

Chapter Fifteen

Xander set the mug of coffee in front of the detective before he sat down opposite with his own cup. Part of him wanted to show the man the door, then go comfort his mate, but he realized she needed some alone time to process what Alex had told her.

"You know she'll be my wife as soon as I can convince her to say yes. All this skilled worker crap won't matter a wink."

Alex sighed before he caught Xander's gaze and held it.

"In my line of work, I see more women in Rachel's position than I care to admit. I can guarantee you only know a fraction of what that bastard did to her. Domestic abuse isn't limited to physical violence. Honestly, from what I've seen, the physical stuff is the fastest to heal. The mental and emotional damage can take years to heal, and in some cases, it never does. I know Rachel is your mate, but even with that connection, you are going to be in for a battle to win her over. A lot of abuse victims suffer PTSD to some extent. She'll have triggers that she won't know she has. You could say or do something and she'll shut down on you. You need to be prepared for it, and when it happens, you need to not lose your head over it. Seeing you get angry, even if it's not aimed at her, is the absolute worst thing you can do for her. Once triggered, a victim reverts back to being in the situation that originally gave them the trigger. She won't be seeing you, but Rocco. She might cringe away from you, beg you stop... or she could lash out, trying to defend herself. It's important you don't take it personally, she's not fighting you, but her memories."

Xander's heart broke for his mate. Why did he wait so long? He'd given that bastard extra months to torment her.

"I'll keep myself in check. Getting her to see Dr Reid regularly is probably a good idea then?"

"If you can, yes. It's going to take time for her to fully heal. To be honest, I'm surprised to see she's agreed to move in with you so soon."

He chuckled without humor. "You underestimate the mating bond. Deep down she feels the connection to me. Mates soothe one another, so when she's close to me, all her hurts lessen. She might not understand why yet, but she craves the peace enough to go with it. I guess it also helped my case that she had no friends from before the fire to call on. If she'd had a good girlfriend, I'm sure she wouldn't be here with me yet."

Alex took a gulp of his coffee before he responded. "Rocco would have made sure that didn't happen. He wouldn't want Rachel to have anyone to turn to. These bastards want their victims to be completely reliant on them."

Fury rushed through his veins. He should have been there to keep her protected earlier than he was. He should have gone looking for her.

"That, right there." Alex was pointing at his clenched fists on the table. "That is what you need to control. Rachel won't see that you're mad at what happened to her, she'll think you're angry with her. She either shut down on you, or she'll run."

Xander huffed out a breath and spread his fingers out against the smooth wood of the table. This was going to be harder than he'd first thought. The very idea of his mate being hurt got him riled, the knowledge she had been. While basically right under his nose? It was almost more than his cat could take. He needed to change the subject. He couldn't focus on this shit at the moment.

"Dominic told me you wanted to talk to me about my team?"

Alex was silent for a few moments, until Xander raised his gaze to look the man in the eye.

"I do. But it can wait until after Jake's funeral. I'm actually waiting on someone to arrive who I need you to meet. He should be here by then. Just make sure you speak with me before you make any moves to head off. I'm not going to stop you or arrest any of you. What I have to discuss with you will help you long-term, give your team some legal clout. So, don't go stressing over it. You have enough to worry about without borrowing trouble."

Xander's phone began ringing and Alex stood.

"I'll head off and let you get back to your mate. See you soon, Xander."

"Okay, thanks for dropping by and for the chat."

As he closed the door behind Alex he answered his phone.

"Hello?"

"Hey, son. Your mother was just wondering when we'd get to meet your mate?"

Xander grinned at his father's gruff voice. He could imagine the hell his mum had been giving the man over not having met her future daughter-in-law yet. Due to complications after his birth, his parents never had any more kids, so it was just him and he got the feeling his mum had missed not having another female around the house all these years.

"How about we come over for dinner tonight?"

"That'd be great. And it curbs how overboard your mother can go with the limited time."

He chatted a bit longer with his father before he hung up. Now, to tell his flighty mate about their dinner plans. Wondering how she was handling everything Alex had dropped on her, on top of everything else, he made his way down the hallway to check on her.

Rachel stared down at Xander's hand, the one he'd just rested on her thigh that had been jerking up and down.

"My folks will adore you. You have no reason to be worried. C'mon, baby girl, take a couple of deep breaths."

Warmth from his palm seeping into her system helped soothe her nerves a little, but she was still stressing about meeting his parents. This was a huge deal. Meeting the parents was a massive step she wasn't sure she was ready for.

She thought back to earlier when Xander had told her. She'd naturally completely lost it and had a panic attack over not having anything nice enough to wear, or any makeup. Xander had given her a strange look and told her his parents wouldn't care what she wore. They wanted to meet her, not her wardrobe. But he didn't understand that it didn't feel right to leave the house dressed so casually. A flash of pain passed over his features before he smiled gently at her and told he'd take her shopping for whatever she needed, that they had plenty of time.

Of course, the man had been true to his word. She hated not having her own money, but he didn't complain or wince at any of her purchases, although he did tell her how he'd never understood the point of makeup. It had been one of best afternoons she'd ever had. Who would ever had thought she'd have such a great time shopping with a man! But she had, and now she sat in Xander's car dressed in a pair of dark blue denim jeans and a pretty short sleeve top. She'd spiked her hair up a little, without making it look like a full on mohawk. She didn't want to borrow trouble, but she didn't want to put forward a false front either. She'd also applied some lip gloss and mascara. Xander telling her how beautiful he thought she was without any make-up had her keeping it light. And honestly, she'd felt a buzz leaving the house without full makeup. Rocco would have a fit if he could see her.

But now all her happiness from earlier had disappeared and she was once again on the verge of bolting away from it all. In a panicked daze, Xander led her from the car to the house. He pulled a key out and let them in, keeping a hand on her lower back. It was the only thing that was keeping her moving forward. She eyed the street for a moment before Xander firmly shut the door with a low growl.

"Stop looking like you want to flee in terror. No one in his house will ever hurt you."

He pressed her back against the door and kissed her silly. Before she could get her brain firing again, she found herself surrounded by Xander's parents, being introduced to the older couple. Ron stood back with an indulgent smile on his face as Bev attempted to squeeze the life out of her with a hug.

"Take it easy, Mum. She needs to breathe."

Rachel chuckled as Bev blushed and mock glared at her son. "Oh, shush you. Just welcoming her to the family. Now come back to the kitchen, dinner is all ready to go."

It was about two hours later, Rachel found herself back in the front seat of Xander's car.

"Your parents are great."

A wide grin spread over his face. "Yeah, Mum can get a bit over-excited with her hugs, but they're the best parents a kid could have asked for."

"Do you have any siblings?"

He'd never spoken of any, but that didn't mean there weren't any other kids.

"Nope. Just me."

"Is this where you tell me you were such a perfect child, they didn't need another?"

His lips ticked up before he got serious. "I wish. After I was born, there were complications that led to Mum losing her uterus. I'm certain if that hadn't happened, I'd have at least half a dozen siblings. That woman was born to be a mother."

Her heart ached for Bev. Rachel had seen how loving and caring the woman was tonight. *She'll be an awesome grandma.* Rachel pressed a hand to her belly. What kind of mother would she be? Did she even want to try?

"Hey, don't look so sad. It was a long time ago and Mum's found ways to cope over the years. She went back to study when I started primary school and got qualified to work with kids. So, for over twenty years now she's worked at a local child care center and is surrounded by babies and little kids five days a week, every week. Trust me, she's happy as a clam with how her life turned out."

They settled into a comfortable silence for the short trip home. No, not home. It was Xander's house. He might have given her the whole 'what's mine is yours' speech, but she didn't have faith in it yet. Couldn't risk believing it. Not yet anyway.

By the time she was following him through the front door, her nerves had returned. She'd had a draining day and now she didn't have a clue about where she was going to sleep, or what Xander expected from her. Rachel really didn't want to have another discussion about her inability to climax, but she did want to cuddle with him.

Xander dumped his wallet and keys in a pot on the kitchen counter and turned to head down the hall. Rachel stayed frozen in place in the middle of the lounge room. Her gaze flicked from his retreating body, to the couch.

"Come here, baby girl."

She hadn't realized he'd come back, but he scooped her up in his arms and after pressing a kiss to her forehead, he carried her down to the bedroom.

"I can see you're getting yourself all worked up over where to sleep. Let me clear it up for you. You sleep with me, in our bed. Each and every night."

She opened her mouth to tell him no way when he gave her a look that had Rachel shutting her mouth before uttering a word.

"Baby girl, I said *sleep*. I don't expect to make love to you every night. I sure as hell wouldn't turn it down, but I don't expect it. With me, you will never have to pay for affection. Do you understand me? If you want to cuddle, come curl up against me and we'll cuddle. The way I see it, sex is a way to show someone you love and care for them, it's not a way to try and make the other person feel those things for you." He paused to stand her at the side of the bed and cup her face in his palms. "I know it's still probably too early for you to believe me, but I do love you, Rachel. From the spikes of your mohawk to the tips of your blue painted toes. So, strip down and hop into bed. Let me hold you close and we'll cuddle, then fall asleep."

Tears welled and she blinked rapidly to hold them back. This giant of a man was impossibly perfect. He'd obviously been thinking during the day about what had happened early this morning and had her pegged. Hell, she hadn't realized that was what she'd been doing, but Xander had it right. She'd been using sex to get the affection she wanted.

For a minute she stayed still and watched as Xander stripped before heading to the bathroom. She began taking her own clothes off when she heard the tap and the sound of an electric toothbrush. She ran her tongue over her own teeth, before concluding she needed to do the same, but she didn't feel comfortable joining him in the bathroom in the buff. She grabbed the t-shirt Xander had been wearing and pulled it over her head. With a smile she inhaled his scent and knew she'd sleep well wearing this. If Xander let her, that is. She padded over to the en suite and pulled out the new toothbrush he'd bought for her, trying hard to not look at the tattooed, naked hunk standing next to her. It seemed strange that she felt closer to him by wearing his shirt. She was about to have the actual man wrapped around her, but his shirt wouldn't roll away from her as he slept. She'd be cocooned in his scent all night long.

Maybe it was a cat-shifter thing.

"You look good in my shirt, baby girl. C'mon, I think your teeth are as clean as they can get."

She rinsed and put her brush away, then Xander took her hand and led her back into the bedroom. He pulled the sheet back and urged her in. She scooted over as he followed her down. Her heart rate kicked up when he wrapped an arm around her waist and pulled her so he was spooned up behind her. She froze, waiting for him to spread her legs and delve his hand between them, or to grope her breasts. When after a minute all he'd done was kiss the top of her head and then settle into the mattress behind her, she finally allowed herself to relax. Of course he was a man of his word. She felt so stupid for doubting him, but she'd been trained to expect certain behavior from men. It was going to take some getting used to, this having a gentleman who wasn't completely self-centered.

With an arm around her waist, Xander kept Rachel close to his side as he took in the gathering crowd. The White family had rented the high school's gymnasium in order to fit everyone in. The entire leap was here, except for the Whites. Jake's immediate family, along with Choden, had spent the morning saying farewell to the man at a private graveside service. They were due any moment at this larger gathering. Xander was glad they'd chosen to celebrate Jake's life, rather than have the entire leap attend the funeral. Guilt still racked him for his part in Jake's death, and he knew Rachel still had nightmares about it all. Rachel moved out of his grip, and his heart warmed when she reached back to snag his palm with hers before she headed to look at the wall of photos that depicted Jake's life.

There were old black and white ones of a happy looking baby and toddler, then colored photographs of him in his school uniform and other childhood activities. Xander chuffed at the photo of Jake at around eighteen, in his fire turnout gear. But there wasn't much yellow left showing. He was covered in soot and mud but had a massive grin on his face and a sparkle in his eyes. Xander felt the same way after they finished containing and extinguishing a fire, especially a big one that took some doing to get it out. It was a thrill only another firefighter truly understood.

"I can't believe he's really gone."

The words slipped out before he thought about the effect they would have. Rachel went stiff beside him and tried to pull her hand free of his. He didn't let her, rather, he pulled her in close to him where he could wrap her up in his arms.

"It's not your fault, Rachel. You know that right?"

Hell, as much as he struggled with his own role in the events that led to Jake losing his life, deep down he knew the fault lay at Rocco's feet. Something happened between the two of them that threw Jake through a floor and left him unable to move. That wasn't something that normally happened at any fire.

Rachel winced before she gave him a tight smile and moved further along the wall of memories. The room was getting crowded by the time they'd made their way to the end where there were photos of Jake throwing a ball for Raksha, Kelly's pet Dalmatian, while Kelly stood nearby laughing. Damn, Jake was going to miss out on even seeing Conner and Tina's baby. His chest felt like someone had taken a sledgehammer to it. It seemed beyond cruel that such a good man had been taken so early in his life. He'd deserved better.

Keeping Rachel close, he glanced around until he spotted his team and a few others from the firehouse. As he made his way over to them, he kept an eye on the people around him. He knew pretty much everyone in the leap—there were a few kids and mates he'd not personally met yet, but aside from those few he knew what everyone in the leap looked like. Therefore, the man standing to attention near the back of the gym stood out. The guy looked military. Between the short, dark hair that showed some gray, the clean shaven face and the way he stood, it was obvious he'd had training. He wore neat casual clothes, but Xander could easily imagine the bloke in Army fatigues.

When he reached his team he brought the guy to their attention.

"Any of you know who that bloke is?"

No one knew, and that worried Xander. Would Trigger be so brazen as to send someone into this ceremony? He looked closely at the man's clothes, looking for bulges that would reveal explosives or weapons. If Trigger were watching what was going on overseas with terrorists, it wouldn't be a huge stretch for them to start sending in suicide bombers. Big enough blast in this one building once the ceremony started would take out the entire leap, and Choden. Well, maybe not Choden. No one was entirely sure how immortal the man was.

Xander and his team were still discussing in hushed voices how they could take the guy out if they needed to when the Whites arrived. The building went silent within moments of their entry, all eyes on them. Choden had an arm around Sophie's shoulders and she dabbed a tissue to her eyes before she glanced around the room. Her head snapped back to the stranger with a look of shock.

"Benny? Is that you?"

The man nodded with a grim expression and Sophie rushed over to embrace him.

"Well, I guess he's not a Trigger then."

Kit stated the obvious before she marched off toward the rest of the White family. Xander and Rachel followed behind and waited their turn to say their condolences. He gave Dominic a quick tight hug.

"I'm so fucking sorry."

"Thanks."

Dominic's voice was rough with emotion and Xander didn't try to get him to say anything more. By the time he'd hugged Adele, Connor, Tina and young Kelly he was barely keeping his tears in check. Rachel had tracks down her cheeks, despite the fact she kept wiping at them with her palms. Sophie pulled her in for a long hug and Xander heard her whisper to his mate that it wasn't her fault. This whole thing was one big nightmare, except for finally having his mate with him.

After he gave Sophie a hug, he stayed close to her.

"Who's Benny?"

A spark flashed in her sad eyes at the mention of his name. "You ever hear about the events that led to Jake coming to Western Australia to save me before he brought me back here?"

Xander shook his head, aware a small crowd was gathering for Sophie's story. "Only know he took a team up to kick Trigger's ass. No details."

A sad little smile curled her lips. "Jake was all alpha even back then. It was only a few months after I'd turned twenty-one when Triggers started attacking my hometown. It was slow to start with—just one or two shifters a night would disappear. But then more Triggers came to town and we all knew how that was going to end. My best friend and her family were gone one morning and my heart broke. My mum had told me about Dream Bonding, how a mate could reach out in their dreams to visit the other."

Xander made a mental note to ask Sophie more about that later. He'd never heard of Dream Bonding, and it sounded like something he could have used with Rachel.

"So when I dreamed of Jake, I knew who he was to me, that he was my mate. As excited as I was to finally see him, I was terrified and grieving. I begged him to come with back up to help save what was left of our town. Naturally, he came running as fast as he could. But it's a long way between Broome and Tasmania. By the time he arrived there were only a handful of us left. We'd holed up in a house and were surrounded."

"And as per usual, Sophie plays down her part." Benny's voice was deep with a gravelly edge to it. He moved to stand in front of Sophie. "Sophie, here, gathered who was left that morning into her family's house. She'd piled the kitchen table with all the weapons she could find, but did she let any of us help? Nope, this crazy-ass alpha woman made us all hide in a bedroom while she went Rambo. The windows had been shot out early that morning, and Sophie spent the day shooting out of them at the Triggers. Managed to keep the bastards at bay, too. Not sure how she managed it but she kept the front and back guarded enough those fuckers didn't dare show their faces."

"You were just a kid, Benny. I couldn't let them get you. And the others, they were all so scared out of their minds, I was worried they'd accidentally shoot themselves in the foot or something."

The man smiled kindly at Sophie. "I was sixteen and more than ready to help take some of those bastards down. But Jake and his boys came in behind them and took care of business. After that we all did our own thing. Sophie, I'm so fucking sorry Trigger got Jake."

Xander stepped back to allow them to hug. If Sophie had grown up with Benny, he was no Trigger. He was a shifter with one hell of an axe to grind against their enemy.

There were so many people and Xander seemed to know all of them. Rachel had never experienced anything like it. He'd told her this was the entire leap, that they were here to celebrate Jake's life and the fact Dominic was being sworn in as Alpha.

Sophie's story had broken her heart. She'd had no idea Triggers were that bad. She'd heard Xander and his team talk about them and what they were known for doing. But that hadn't seemed real. Sophie and Benny's first-hand account was extremely real. Trigger had taken out all but a handful of their leap. It was genocide. Anger had lit her up and she'd trembled with it, as she had no way of venting it.

Xander had pulled her in close and pressed a kiss to the top of her head. She doubted he understood why she was shaking, but the fact he noticed and wanted to comfort her helped her gain some control.

Now she sat between Xander and Kit a few rows from the front of the gym. Good thing the local high school had recently upgraded their gymnasium. If not, she wasn't sure where they would have done this. Not many places could accommodate what had to be close to a thousand people. She shook her head when she realized that nearly everyone here was a shifter. Too strange.

Kit leaned over to whisper to her. "You doing okay, Rach?"

"Yeah, just trying to wrap my head around this shifter thing and the fact that most of the people in this room aren't actually people."

Kit chuckled for a second, before she frowned over at her. "You shifted yet?"

She winced and shook her head. She'd been too scared. What if she got stuck as a leopard and couldn't change back?

"You need to before Choden leaves. Until you've fully shifted, then returned to human, we won't know if he completely undid whatever your parents had done. This is important, Rach. Your leopard needs air time. If you hold off too long, you'll end up shifting by accident when you're under extreme pressure or experiencing an intense emotion. Look, if you're not comfortable doing it with Xander, I can do it with you."

Rachel screwed her nose up. "No offense Kit, but I don't need to see you naked."

The woman didn't have an ounce of fat on her. Rachel was fairly certain the woman's ass didn't even giggle when she ran. So unfair.

Before Kit could say anything more, Choden stood on the stage at the front of the building and raised both his hands, palms facing the crowd. Silence was nearly instant and Rachel marveled at the quietness, especially considering how many were here. He lowered his hands before he began to speak in the careful, articulate way he always seemed to.

"We are gathered here for two purposes. Firstly, to say farewell to our brother, Jake White, who was buried this morning. He was an amazing man of many talents and was a fair and just Alpha of this leap for many years. It saddens my heart and soul that he has been taken from us so soon." The old monk paused to clear his throat. It was clear he did indeed feel the loss deeply. "Around the room you will find photos and notes from various people about their memories of this great man. I ask that you all take the time to read and look at each one, talk to your leap brothers and sisters about how he helped you. The best way to carry on his memory is to pay it forward. Jake helped many, many people—shifter or human, he did not discriminate. Any he could help, he did."

Kit sniffled and Jessie wrapped his arm around her shoulders pulling her in closer to him. Rachel looked around and noticed a lot of couples were in a similar pose.

She'd only spoken briefly a few times with Jake, but he'd been nice and had always smiled at her. The last time she saw him filled her mind. He'd come in with Xander, just barged straight into a burning building without a second thought. To rescue her. Both of them could have been killed, hell, her and Rocco too. Lighting that fire was the single dumbest thing she'd ever done. Tears pricked her eyes at the price her stupidity had cost everyone.

"I'm sorry."

She whispered as quietly as she could, but Xander still heard her. Damn his super sensitive hearing. He pulled her over until she was sitting on his lap. He tucked her in against him so her head was on his shoulder, before he quietly spoke to her.

"Don't. It's not your fault. You did what you had to do to escape, nothing more. If Rocco hadn't locked you in, you wouldn't have lit that fire. No matter how you look at this, Jake's death is on his hands, no one else's."

She understood what Xander was saying, but the guilt wouldn't go away. Maybe she shouldn't have come today? It was too late now. She couldn't leave, but she did her best to not focus on the stories that were being shared by various people. Instead, she shuffled down so her ear was against Xander's chest. His heartbeat was loud and strong and she closed her eyes and focused on it, breathing slowly and evenly as she tried to empty her mind of all the swirling thoughts and the guilt.

"Hey, baby girl. You'll want to see this."

Her cheeks heated as she realized she'd drifted off to

sleep. She turned to face the stage to see Dominic kneeling with his head bowed as Choden stood before him, chanting in a language she'd never heard before.

"Choden is raising Dominic to Alpha of the leap."

She was glad Xander explained without her having to ask. Awestruck, Rachel didn't move, barely even breathed as Choden performed a ceremony that was filled with Tibetan beauty. Each time he chanted, she felt something deep within her ease and a sense of peace flow through her. So much so, that by the time he'd finished on the stage, Rachel was completely at ease.

Chapter Sixteen

Three days later Xander sat with his team and Dominic in the meeting room at the firehouse. He sipped his coffee as he waited for Alex to arrive, along with his mysterious guest.

"When did they say they'd be here?"

Dominic glanced at his watch before answering Joel. "Any minute now."

Xander wished they'd hurry up. Once they got this part over with, his team needed to discuss what the boys had learned about Rocco's location. He clenched and released his fists a couple of times. He had to make sure that bastard was in the ground before they left for the mainland. He knew Kit was getting edgy, wanting to go see if the intel on her mother's current location was correct. Xander could understand where she was coming from. She hadn't seen the woman since her fifteenth birthday, and still wasn't one hundred percent sure her father hadn't had her murdered.

Then there was the other reason he was wanting to get things moving. As much as he wanted to be here, planning his team's strategy, he didn't like that he'd been forced to leave Rachel home alone. Unfortunately, everyone who she could have spent the day with was working. The only one who could have done it was Tina, but she was heavily pregnant and reeling over the loss of Jake. Not what Rachel needed to be exposed to at this point. Xander could easily tell she still blamed herself for his death. He'd tried to get her to come and hang out in the station with him, but she'd refused. Told him her days of being told when, where, and how to live were over. He winced. Dammit, he just wanted to keep her safe until he was certain Rocco wouldn't come after her, but he wouldn't contain her like he wanted to. She was still rediscovering her backbone and spirit from all Rocco had done to her. He couldn't risk sending her spiraling back down into a hole. He loved her too much to risk her mental health like that.

Noise in the hallway pulled him from his thoughts and he turned to watch Alex stroll through the door, followed by Benny. What the hell? Xander frowned at the man.

"What does Benny have to do with any of this?"

Dominic spoke Xander's thoughts. Benny winced at his name. "Please, call me Sawyer. Sophie is the only one allowed to call me by my childhood nickname. I'd prefer she didn't either, but she won't listen."

"Yeah, Mum's like that. Still doesn't answer my question. I thought it was strange to see you there yesterday."

Alex cleared his throat. "How about we all sit down and I'll explain." He paused long enough for them all to take a seat. "Right, let me start by saying I have no intention of arresting anyone for anything that is spoken of in this meeting. Jake always kept me in the loop with what was going down. In case things went south, I could step in to help, if I could. That means I know about your team and its purpose, and I can take a guess at what went down in Hobart with all the animal attacks. I'll let Sawyer introduce himself and explain what we'd like to happen. It's taken a lot of work for Sawyer to get where he is, and when I caught wind of his skills, my instincts screamed he wasn't fully human. Lucky for all of us, I was right and when I approached him, it turns out our ideas were very similar. So, I'll hand this over to Sergeant Benjamin Sawyer to tell you his plan."

Xander raised his eyebrows. Sergeant? He'd thought the man looked military, but a Sergeant? Bloody hell.

"Morning, all. You know my name already, and I assume you all heard Sophie explain my history in regards to her and Jake?" Xander and the others all nodded. "What you don't know is, I lost my parents in that Trigger raid, and I swore I'd do all I could to wipe out those bastards. Along with another young man orphaned on that day, we joined the Army. Since then, we've both done all we could to work our way up the ranks to get where we are now—which is in the position to be able to bring in your team as a special ops team. You would all need to pass some physical and written tests, but I can't imagine you'll have any difficulty with passing any of it. Your main purpose would be to track and capture Triggers, and any other threat to shifters. I understand you'll also keep your ear to the ground for Lost Ones, which is fine with us, but it won't be your main focus. You will be paid for it, and you'll have the backing of the Australian Army if you get in trouble. Okay, I've put my cards on the table, you know what I'm offering, and you know my motivation for wanting this. Now, it's your turn. Tell me what you've managed to do in the last six months with your influx of Triggers here in Tasmania."

Xander glanced around at his team, then over to Dominic before he spoke to Alex and Sawyer. "Can we have five minutes to talk this over with our Alpha?"

Sawyer nodded and abruptly turned and left. Yep, that boy was one hundred percent military. Alex followed, and before he closed the door spoke. "We'll just be here in the hall, give us a yell when you want us to come back in."

The moment they were alone, Xander turned to Dominic. "Can we trust him?"

Dominic sighed before crossing his arms over his chest. "Talk about throwing me in the bloody deep end. Look, Alex has always taken care of us and he knows damn well we're responsible for those deaths in Hobart. I think that's as solid a sign of trust as we're ever going to get, and Mum's told us before about what happened that day up in her hometown. Sawyer has one hell of an axe to grind with Trigger. I'll check in with Choden before I go letting him take you anywhere, but my instincts say he's being honest with us. We tell him about the farmhouse here in Rosebery and Hobart. Not sure if Alex has told him about Nick, but we'll soon find out."

Xander turned to Kit. "You want to explain about the farmhouse? And I'll cover Hobart?"

Kit had tensed in her posture but she shrugged one shoulder and agreed.

"Right, well, let's bring them back in."

With a smile Rachel looked around herself as she walked down the street. This was amazing. She was outside on her own. No car trailing her, no thugs following at a distance. It was just her and the rest of the world. She took a deep breath and enjoyed the fresh, clean country air filling her lungs. Hobart wasn't a huge city, but it was still a lot more crowded than Rosebery.

With a spring in her step, she headed toward the bank. Thankfully her bank had a branch here and now that she had her passport, she should be able to access her account to draw some cash and order a new bank card. Xander was being extremely generous, but Rachel wanted to stand on her own two feet. She needed to. Rocco had robbed her of so much, she hadn't realized the extent until she was free. Rachel couldn't work out how it happened. Growing up she'd been raised to be her own person, to not let others tread on her. But somehow Rocco had slipped past her guard, dug in deep, and hollowed her out. That reminded her, she needed to make sure he didn't have access to her bank account. She hadn't given him a card, but she had no idea if he'd managed to find some other way to gain access.

Shaking herself free of any thoughts of that bastard, she pushed open the door and winced at the blast of air conditioning that hit her square in the face. Rubbing her arms to ease the sudden chill, she headed over to wait to see a teller. Ah, the joy of country banks, short lines and friendly service. In under an hour Rachel was back out on the sidewalk, cash and a new card in her pocket, on the way to Xander's house.

Her next stop was to get a new purse and handbag. She'd discovered it was all these little items she used every day that she missed most. Kind of funny really, she'd never paid much attention to most things she used all the time. She couldn't have said what color her hair brush had been...but she sure as hell knew how much she missed it after the fire.

With nothing much else on her agenda to do with her day, she spent ages going over every purse and bag in the shop before she settled on ones she thought would suit her best. The purse was a fairly small one that she'd be able to tuck into her front jeans pocket if she wanted to. It was a deep blue color that made her think of the ocean. The bag she settled on was a medium sized one she'd be able to fit her phone, a water bottle and a book in easily and she could sling it over her shoulder or wear it across her body.

Once she made her purchases, she asked the assistant if she could cut all the tags off for her, then spent a few minutes sorting it all out before putting the bag over her head so it sat across her body. She felt more normal walking out of the store. It was strange how bare she'd felt without a purse to carry around.

Glancing at her phone for the time, she figured at two in the afternoon the bulk of the lunch rush would be over at Top Pub by now. She wanted to talk to someone about that job she'd seen advertised there last week. She doubted in such a small town that the position would have been filled already. Before she started the three block walk, she ducked into a corner store to grab a bottle of water. It wasn't the height of summer anymore, but February in Australia was still pretty hot, even down here in Tassie.

Rachel was so busy enjoying her freedom, she didn't realize it was at risk until a thick arm wrapped around her chest at the same time a hard object was jammed against her side.

"Don't make any sudden moves, pet. I have no issue Tasering you."

Fuck. Rocco. Why did he even care where she was? She'd thought he'd move on with one of his dancers and never think about her again. He'd made it pretty clear he didn't give a shit about her.

"Why are you even here? What do you want?"

He scoffed at her as he led her down a side street away from the main road. She'd walked away from the shops where all the people were, but surely someone in a car saw Rocco grab her before he got her out of sight?

"Eleven days away from me and look at you. No makeup, hair a mess...and what the fuck are you wearing?"

Tears pricked her eyes. She'd been confident she looked good when she left this morning. Hell, Xander had taken one look at her and kissed her until her head spun. Then with a growl he pulled himself away from her, cursing that he had a meeting and couldn't stay home with her all day. She'd had lip gloss on before that. Not that Rocco counted that as makeup.

"You're not the boss of me anymore. I can do and wear whatever the bloody hell I want."

A groan left her when he jammed the Taser harder against her ribs.

"I will hurt you. If you make me do it before we get to the car, you'll really suffer. In fact, do that, and I might not let you wake up ever again."

Her flash of bravery was over and with tears pricking her eyes, she didn't say a thing or try to fight him as he led her to his car that sat alone on a back street. She'd survived many of his moods by placating him, so that's what she tried to work out how to do now. Before she came up with anything to say to him, sirens filled the air. Rachel sent a silent prayer that someone had seen her being taken and called them. It wasn't like Rosebery was a hotbed of criminal activity. Surely they were coming for her.

"Fuckin' hell."

Before she knew what he was up to, he opened the trunk and pushed her forward so she fell into the small space. She put her arms out to catch herself but before she could get any leverage, Rocco lifted her legs, shoved her in and closed the lid.

She whimpered as the light disappeared and she was left in complete darkness. Her thoughts swirled as she found herself reliving Rocco beating her. Her body jerked and twitched with each blow and kick. She covered her head and curled into a ball against the onslaught. Then she slid forward and hit the top of her head on something solid, but not hard like a wall. She patted her hand around her to find carpet. Where was she? Shit. In the damn boot. She'd had a flashback and what shitty timing for it too. Jennifer had warned her she may get PTSD from the abuse, but this was the first full on flash back she'd had. It had seemed so real.

But now she was fully aware of where she was and remembering seeing something on TV about what to do if you get stuck in a car trunk. Moving her fingers around she tried to find the corner where the lights would be. She needed to knock them out so she could wave at cars around her. After a few minutes of finding nothing but smooth carpet, she had to admit defeat on that front. Apparently this car didn't have easy access to the tail lights.

She continued her search around until she found a small ring on a cord. Bingo! That would push down the back seat into the car. But that wouldn't help her while Rocco was driving. She didn't want him to Taser her. She had a bad feeling about how much worse he'd hurt her if she couldn't defend herself at all.

With a finger through the loop she waited until she felt the car come to a stop. The moment she heard a door open she yanked on that thing with all she had. The center part of the seat fell forward and she didn't waste a moment wriggling through, into the back seat. She just had her legs through when the boot opened and Rocco let loose a string of curses. As fast as she could she fumbled with the door handle to get out. When the door opened she burst forward and took a whole two steps before her body lit up like a firecracker. *Fuck that hurt.*

For the past ten minutes Xander had been feeling off. He couldn't pinpoint what was wrong, but he knew something was. He struggled to concentrate as Sawyer told them about the testing they'd need to pass to be brought in as a Special Forces team.

He loved the idea of making their team part of the Army. It would make what they were doing legal, give them backing if they got in trouble and it would pay them so they wouldn't need to find and keep day jobs while they hunted. It was also a way for Rachel to stay in Australia. Kit had already agreed to work with her so she would be ready to pass the testing and Sawyer had said that new members of the team could join at any time. He'd personally come down to oversee the testing whenever they needed him to. Being a shifter, he understood that eventually they'd all find their mates and hopefully, those mates would have skills to benefit the team. Rachel being a chef worked out well for them. Xander also suspected that Sawyer's long term plan included more than one team.

Unable to sit still, Xander rose and paced across the room. He rubbed the knuckles of his right hand over his heart before he ran his left palm over the back of his neck. Where the hell was all this tension coming from? With a growl he rolled his shoulders and kept pacing.

"Xander!"

The way Dominic barked his name had him thinking it wasn't the first attempt the man had made to get his attention. He froze and looked toward him, noting that the entire room was silent and all eyes were on him.

"Sorry, I don't—"

Sudden intense pain shot through his body as though he'd been hit by lightning. He threw his arm out to brace against the wall as his knees went loose.

"Fuck. Rachel."

Moments later when all the discomfort and agony vanished, clarity came in an instant. He'd been feeling his mate's emotions, then her pain. Now that he felt nothing from her he was petrified. Ignoring the voices around him, he closed his eyes and focused on her, trying to get a sense she was still alive. After what felt like forever, his instincts finally kicked in and told him she was alive but unconscious.

Pushing himself off the wall, he opened his eyes to focus on those in the room with him. Alex was on his phone making demands about a recent emergency call. Sawyer stood in front of him, silently waiting for him to zone back in.

"You back with us?" Xander nodded. "Good. Tell us what she was planning on doing today."

Still trying to get his thoughts straight, Xander took a moment to remember what she'd told him this morning.

"She was going to go to the bank in town to sort out a new card, then I think she was going to wander around the main street relaxing." He looked Sawyer directly in the eyes. "She could be anywhere, and I'm certain she's now unconscious."

"Rocco has her."

Alex's deep voice silenced the room and Xander fell back against the wall. "How do you know?"

"He grabbed her on the street about twenty minutes ago and a civilian called emergency when she saw it happen. A patrol car was sent out there, but they couldn't find anything. The woman that called it in, followed at a distance and managed to get the plate number of the car he tossed Rachel in. It's registered to him. Not that it helps a great deal, Classic Convicts is his registered home so no idea where he'd be with her."

"She has her phone with her, I made sure she took it this morning. Can we use the GPS in that to locate her?"

Before Alex could answer him, his own phone started ringing. With a sense of foreboding, he pulled it from his pocket to see it was Rachel's phone calling him.

"It's her phone."

"Doubt it's her calling though." Kit's voice had gone low and dark. She was pissed. Rachel was her friend, they'd bonded over doing all that laundry.

Holding in a deep breath, he answered and put it on speaker.

"Hello?"

"Let's keep this short. I have your mate. You want her back? Come get her. Alone. I'm at the little caravan park just outside of town. You know the place?"

"Yeah, I know it."

"Good. I'll see you soon then. Remember, alone. Or I'll start cutting up my little pet here."

The bastard hung up and Xander let loose a growl as he

clenched his fists tight enough his knuckles made a few cracking sounds.

"That's where Barbara's body was found."

Xander flicked his gaze to Alex. Barbara had been Robyn's sidekick in her sick plans to trap Dale into a relationship by holding his daughter, Tina hostage. Thankfully that situation all worked out and Conner and Tina were now happily mated.

"You give me a ten-minute head start. I don't want to risk him hurting her more than he already has, but I'm not stupid enough to believe this isn't a well laid out trap."

He didn't give any of them time to respond. He snatched up his phone and headed out the door. He had a mate to save, and this time he'd do it right and kill that fucker Rocco, so he couldn't ever come back to hurt any of them again.

It didn't take long for him to drive to the tiny park set back in the scrub. It was so far off the main roads, not many tourists used it. Rosebery was too far away for the ones that wanted the Cradle Mountain experience, and not close enough to the Hobart or Launceston for the city slickers that just wanted a small taste of the Australian wilderness. He had no idea how the owners kept the place open and running. Although, it wasn't like they paid much attention to it. The cabins were run down and they didn't exactly do regular checks, as proven by psychotic Robyn staying here for who knew how long while the police were looking for her. Hell, Barbara had been dead about a week before her body was found, or so he'd heard.

Clearing his mind of all that shit, he pulled up away from the only cabin that had a car beside it. This was it. He had no idea what he was about to walk in on. He'd started feeling Rachel's stress about five minutes ago so he knew his mate was awake.

He hoped Rocco hadn't heard him pull in. Taking a deep breath, he slid out of his car and closed it up as quietly as he could. On light feet he jogged over to the cabin. Approaching the side, he carefully moved so he could see inside without showing his full face to anyone who might be looking out. What he saw had his blood running cold. Rachel was tied spread eagle on the bed. It looked to him like Rocco had used strips of the bedsheet to bind her. Rocco stood over her with his hands on his hips. Xander honed his hearing in through the glass.

"So nice of you to wake up, pet. Would have been nicer ten minutes ago so I didn't have carry your fat ass in here."

He leaned down and she whimpered as he ripped at her pants, pulling them down to reveal her hip bones.

"Dammit. I thought you were his mate. What? You can't even get a shifter to claim you when you were made for him? Fucking useless as usual. Bet he doesn't even show up to save your ass. *Fuck.*"

Clearly enraged, Rocco backhanded her before he stormed away to the kitchen area of the room. Tamping down his fury at watching his mate be assaulted, Xander kicked his own ass for not forcing Rachel to learn how to shift. She'd been scared and he figured they had time to work on her fears before she had to shift. But if he had pushed her, she'd be able to break free now. If Rocco had used rope or cuffs, she'd be stuck, but those scraps of sheet would tear away easily if she shifted forms.

He was trying to work out a way to sneak in somehow when Rocco came back into his line of sight with a fucking knife. His vision took on a red haze and he bolted for the door. No way was that bastard cutting up his mate.

It was as though she'd woken up in the middle of a horror movie. Rachel hadn't really fully come to until Rocco had started pulling her pants down. She may have had sex with him in the past, but now she'd experienced Xander's loving caresses, the very thought of Rocco's touch was enough to make her stomach turn. The feel of his fingers scraping against her skin made bile rise up her throat.

"Dammit. I thought you were his mate. What? You can't even get a shifter to claim you when you were made for him? Fucking useless as usual. Bet he doesn't even show up to save your ass. *Fuck.*"

His face went red with rage and Rachel cringed, knowing he was seconds from losing his temper and hitting her. Rocco's backhand had her head snapping to the side. Her cheek throbbed and a muscle in her neck twinged as though she'd pulled the damn thing. Blinking away tears, she saw him stomp away from her to the kitchen.

With his back turned she tugged at her wrists and ankles but the binds held firm. She was about to try to twist her hands to free them when he turned back toward her. Her reprieve was over. More tears pricked her eyes and she whimpered when he came back to her with a large kitchen knife in one hand. She'd gotten free of this bastard once already; this shit shouldn't be happening to her now!

"He'll come for me. I promise he will. Just because we haven't completed the mating yet, doesn't mean he's rejected me."

Xander had never said anything about leaving her, or not accepting her. Hell, he knew she wasn't looking for a relationship but had still opened his home to her. He also hadn't pressured her to have sex again after that first time. That thought had her frowning. Was that a sign he was going to kick her to the curb?

Thankfully, before she could follow through on that train of thought the cabin door burst open with a loud crash and there he stood, her fierce guardian come to rescue her. She relaxed back against the mattress with a sigh of relief as she drank in the sight of him. He was clearly furious and had his lethal gaze locked onto Rocco.

"Ah, so you haven't given up on her after all."

Rocco tossed the knife on the table near the bed before he reached a hand behind himself to grab something. Rachel's eyes tracked his movement and she gasped when she saw him pull free a Taser that had been tucked into the back of his pants.

"I was planning to have someone here to video this, but the bastard did a runner on me. No doubt to the higher ups to claim my discovery. Asshole."

Xander didn't say a word, only growled low and mean

before a blue ball formed around him. Her breath caught in her throat. He was shifting, something deep within her perked up and took notice. Just like the time back in that hospital room when he'd shown her what he was.

Rocco was fast as he discharged the weapon toward Xander. The moment the pins touched the blue sphere Xander yelled out in pain and was blasted out of the bubble of light. A scream tore free from her throat as he crashed back against the wall and lay motionless.

"Just like last time, worked a treat."

She couldn't stand to hear one more word from that bastard's mouth. Her body vibrated with rage and grief and before she knew what was happening she heard material ripping, then all she could see was blue. Oh hell, she was shifting! After two seconds of panic, she pushed her conscious energy into the process. She needed the teeth and claws of her leopard to take down Rocco. Thank fuck Tasers only had one shot per charge. No way did Rocco have time to reload and shoot before she'd be a snow leopard. It had taken Xander under a minute to shift that one time she'd seen him.

As the blue cleared she saw Rocco's shocked expression and smiled. *Didn't know I could do this, did you asshole?* She knew he couldn't hear her but she didn't care. Felt good to say it, even if it was only in her head. Rocco's face had lost all color and he scrambled toward the door. No way was he leaving here alive. She happily allowed her new animal instincts to take over and stalked quickly after him. Once in range, she pounced with a growl and took the bastard down. Digging her claws into each of his shoulders, she heard him howl and thrash beneath her, then she wrapped her mouth around the front of his throat and tore it free. His body stilled as she spat out the mouthful of blood and flesh next to him. Gah, he tasted terrible.

Jumping free of his body, she bounded over to Xander's still form. He was on his side up against the wall. When she noticed his chest rise and fall, relief flowed through her. Nothing else was moving, but his eyes were open and he stared at her. She focused on his gaze and saw what she thought was pride and love.

She laid her big body down next to him so she was touching him as much as possible. He still didn't move but the contact helped soothe her. She wasn't entirely sure how to get back to human, and her mind was still jacked up on adrenaline, so she couldn't focus to try. With a whimper she licked at his bicep before pressing the side of her face against his chest. *Please get up, Xander. Please, please. Be alright, and get up.*

"Bloody hell!"

Baring her teeth she swung her head toward the doorway and who ever had spoken. Dominic stood gripping the door frame with one hand and the other scrubbing his hair roughly as he frowned over at her. Then he faced away from the cabin, took a deep breath, and called out.

"Kit! Call Adele then grab your spare set of clothes and get in here fast." He then took a step inside toward her. "It's okay, Rachel. You did good, honey. I'm so proud of you, but we need to help Xander and we can't if you're blocking him from us. Nor can we have medical people in here with you in your leopard form. Can you shift back for me?"

Rachel pressed against Xander a little more and whimpered. Her thoughts spun and she closed her eyes against the pain banging around her skull. Then Kit was there, her fingers in her fur as her voice filled her mind.

"Hey, girl. So you finally shifted, huh? I know you've probably got a headache from hell, but I'm going to need you to focus. The men have all left and I've got some clothes for you to wear, okay? So help me out here and focus on what you look like as a human. Roll away from Xander so we don't hurt him anymore. That's the girl. Now, close your eyes and picture it. Imagine wriggling your fingers and toes—that's it."

Rachel took a shuddering breath and opened her eyes to see Kit smiling gently at her.

"Is it always like that?"

Kit shook her head. "No. Your leopard's been locked away for too long and she broke free with force. It shouldn't ever hurt like that. Now, let's get you dressed before Adele arrives with the ambulance." Remembering that Xander needed help had her dressing in record time before spinning back around to check him. His dark brown gaze was still locked on her, and his big body remained unmoving. She crawled over to him and softly caressed his cheek.

"Be careful not to move him. If he has a spinal injury we could make it worse."

Kit's warning had her pulling her hand away carefully. Tears poured down her cheeks but she ignored them. What was wrong with him? Dominic crouched down beside her.

"What the fuck happened here? I've never seen anything like it"

"We have." Rachel didn't look away from Xander but knew that it was Joel speaking. "He looks like Jake did after he came through the floor. He can't move his body, but his eyes are responsive and he's still breathing. Even though he can't move his limbs, they're not locked up. We had no trouble moving Jake, we just couldn't get to him fast enough."

Pain made Joel's voice rough and it tore at her heart. Since her head still pounded with a wicked headache she spoke quietly. "Rocco hit him with a Taser, mid-shift. It blasted him out of the ball of blue light and he landed here like this."

Sirens filled the air, then people were everywhere. Kit pulled her into her arms and held her as she watched in horror while Xander was prepared, then moved to a stretcher.

"Choden will know what to do, sweetie. Your mate's too strong to go down this easy."

Rachel knew Kit was trying to be reassuring but she'd heard stories of how strong Jake had been. And he'd gone down exactly like this.

Chapter Seventeen

Hours later, Rachel sat curled up in an uncomfortable hospital chair—one of the ones that folded out into a single bed. The thing sucked as a chair and Rachel doubted it would function any better as a bed. With a shallow breath, she tightened her arms around her legs, pulling her knees tighter in against her chest. The room was getting crowded, but everyone was careful to not block her view of the hospital bed.

Dr Maynard, who was another human who knew about shifters, couldn't find anything wrong with Xander. Apparently there was no reason for him to not be moving, but he wasn't. Adele, Dominic's mate who was a shifter and a paramedic, had gently turned Xander's head so he faced her a while ago, so now Rachel sat, with her gaze locked with his. She could clearly read his fear, and she was sure he saw the same thing in her eyes.

The room suddenly went silent and she flicked her gaze over to see who'd come in now. She wasn't sure there was any room for anyone else. Xander's parents were here, as was his team. Dominic and Adele, that Benny guy from the funeral, and Alex, the detective who'd given her back her passport, was standing next to him.

Choden entered the room in that steady, smooth way he always did and people moved out of his way, allowing him quick passage to Xander's side. She unfolded from her seat and moved to stand beside Xander, taking his hand in hers out of reflex. He, of course, didn't return her grip, but it still soothed her to be in contact with him.

"Please, can you help him?"

Her voice was rough, both with emotion and from screaming back at the cabin. Choden gave her a gentle smile before he laid his palms on either side of Xander's face. He began chanting. It was similar to what he'd done at the Alpha Ceremony, but not the same.

She held her breath, waiting for something to happen. After a minute, nothing had changed, and tears filled her eyes again and she sucked in a breath. She knew she'd told Xander she didn't want to be in another relationship so soon, but the thought of never feeling Xander's touch again or hearing his deep voice cut her all the way to her soul. Suddenly she knew that holding Xander at arm's length was simply letting Rocco win again. She refused to allow that. She'd killed him herself, she knew he was gone for good. She would not let him hold her back from living her life for another moment.

If only Xander would come back to her.

After what felt like hours, but was probably only fifteen or twenty minutes, something brushed against her palm. With a gasp she looked down and saw Xander's fingertip twitching against her hand. She did nothing to stop her tears or her laugh.

"He's moving! His finger is moving!"

It was like she'd popped the tension in the room and everyone relaxed. Choden kept his palms on Xander's face and his chanting never stopped filling the air. Over the next ten minutes Xander's arms and legs began twitching and jerking. After thirty minutes, Choden stopped and stepped back. Rachel gasped when Xander sat up in a flash and snatched her against him, dragging her into his lap. She wrapped her arms around his neck and buried her face against his shoulder as she sobbed in relief. Her man was back. He shuddered, then pressed kisses over her face.

"Dominic, in the future, if this happens and I am not close by. A low level electric shock should reverse the effects. I would suggest getting some low wattage Tasers to keep around the place. It will be agony on the shifter to do it that way, so if at all possible, call for me."

Rachel winced, glad Choden had been available to them. She wasn't sure she could have withstood seeing Xander go through more pain.

"Thank you, Choden. I appreciate you helping me. Now, if everyone could please leave, I need some privacy with my mate."

Her face heated with a blush as everyone filed out chuckling. Once the door clicked shut, Xander's chest vibrated with a low growl for a moment before she found his mouth on hers. His kisses were deadly, and this one was the most powerful he'd ever given her. Her mind emptied and all the tension she'd been hanging onto rolled out from her body to leave her relaxed and content by the time he lifted his face from hers.

"You scared the shit out of me, baby girl. You're not allowed to ever get kidnapped again."

She smiled at him and cocked an eyebrow up. "And I just had my 'please kidnap me' shirt arrive. What ever will I do with that now?"

He shook his head with a chuckle. "Yeah, I get it. You didn't chose it. *Smart-ass*." His expression grew serious as he framed her face with his large palms. "While my body didn't work, and my eyes were blurry, my ears functioned perfectly. I'm so proud of you, Rachel. You were all warrior and saved both our asses in that cabin."

All humor fled and her eyes filled with tears. Dammit, she hated all this crying crap. "I was so scared he'd killed you. My leopard rose up and I sort of just followed her instincts. Human me had no clue what to do."

"I'd really like for the human you to get trained up. I want you to be able to walk into anyplace confident, because you know you can kick ass and get yourself out if you have to."

Rachel frowned, her thoughts churning. "You're not talking about me taking a couple of self-defense classes are you? What are you really asking me here?"

Xander looked into her eyes, trying to work out what her reaction would be. Ultimately he knew he had no way of knowing until he asked.

"I'm asking you to join my team and help hunt Trigger." He pressed a finger over her lips to stop her from speaking.

"Please, let me finish, then you can tell me what you want to do. Okay?" She continued to frown but nodded. "We won't just be tracking them, we'll also be looking for Lost Ones—shifters that don't have a leap supporting them. Shifters like Kit, who got kicked out of her home before she knew what she was. These shifters are lost, and often they're struggling to survive. But the main reason behind our team's creation was to go on the offensive to track and deal with Triggers. Triggers have been attacking leaps for a damn long time. Pretty much every shifter has been touched in some way by Trigger violence. We've been lucky here in Tassie. We hadn't ever seen them. Then last year we found ourselves with a cell of them. They were specifically targeting Kit when they got Nick. Kit led the charge to take them out, but we missed some. Jake was sick of shifters always being the victims. As I've said before, due to the way we were created, we're protective by nature. We don't look for trouble, but we have no issue defending ourselves if trouble finds us. Jake thought we could turn the tables on them, even the score. Nick was my leap brother, we grew up together. Of course I wanted vengeance for his death. But on top of that, it gave me somewhere to belong. A job that fit me. I'm an alpha male, but I have no desire in challenging Dominic for the leadership of the entire leap. Leading this team? It calms my leopard and gives me purpose."

He paused to lean in to kiss her forehead. He loved how she softened whenever he did it.

"But I love you, Rachel. Leading the team will be empty

if you're not standing by my side. Hobart was a test run, to see how we function. Our next mission is in South Australia. We're going to track down Kit's mum, see if we can find any lost ones and deal with any Triggers we find on our way. Not only do I need you, but the team needs you. None of us are real skilled in the cooking department. Jake was careful with who he chose. Joel and Jordan are our tech. Kit is our fighter—her father was a martial arts expert, and she has taught the rest of us what she knows. Jessie's a professional rally driver and can drive anything, anywhere, and he's damn fast. Sean is great with puzzles, putting information together and seeing what's underneath it all. So, what do you say? Are you willing to join us? Make sure we don't starve?"

She took a deep breath and stared at him, making him nervous. He hoped he hadn't overplayed his hand. If she bolted, he'd follow. He would never give up on her. But he didn't want to lose the team either. He moved his hands to stroke over her neck and shoulders, then down her arms.

"What do you do when you find a Trigger? I know I've just killed one, but I'm not happy supporting a team that is slaughtering people all the time. There has to be another way."

"Well, we didn't have a choice until today. It was a case of us or them. And they sure as hell have no issue killing entire leaps when they find them. But that's why Sawyer is here." She gave him a blank look. "Benny, from the funeral? His name is Sawyer. Sophie is the only one who gets away with calling him Benny apparently. Anyhow,

Sawyer is a Sergeant in the Australian Army. At the meeting earlier today he put forward an offer for us. One that means the team would become a Special Forces unit with full Army backing. He's going to oversee our testing to get us through the entrance stuff, then we'll report directly to him. That means, when we find Triggers, if we can capture them, we call in Sawyer to come take them away. So we're not going to be running around the country slaughtering Triggers. It also has the benefit that the government will pay us to do our job, so we won't have to find work as we go about our search."

She lifted her hands and Xander groaned when her soft fingers trailed over his face. He loved having her touch him, her gentle caresses were divine.

"What if we never manage to complete the mating? Will you be okay if I'm not wearing your mark?"

The thought of marking her had his body hardening.

"I've got some ideas on how we can complete the mating, but if we can't ever get there, it won't change a thing for me. I love you. Are you saying you want that? To be my mate?"

Frowning she wriggled against his erection, making him moan.

"I thought I was your mate. I didn't realize I had a choice."

He swallowed past the lump that had suddenly formed in his throat.

"You always have a choice, baby girl. We were born to be together, but it doesn't force us. If you don't want to be mine for the rest of our lives, you can walk away. It'll kill me, and I don't think I'll ever stop trying to convince you to have me as yours. I know I'll never take another, no matter what you decide, Rachel. You'll always have my heart."

A small smile tugged at her mouth before she leaned in and pressed her lips against his. It was a sweet brush of a kiss, then she pulled back and whispered. "Ask me again."

He ran his fingers through the short hair on the sides of her head, holding her firmly.

"Rachel, will you marry me, complete our mating and travel with me and the team? Be mine for the rest of our days."

Her eyes sparkled and her lips curled into a full grin. "Yes, I'd love to be your wife and mate. Even if we can't complete it, you've well and truly claimed my heart."

His heart pounded against his ribs as he pulled her in and took her mouth. No soft brush this time —no, this kiss was full of heat and passion. He couldn't wait to be discharged so he could take his mate home to their bed.

Time passed in a blur for Rachel, as Xander was released, then Dominic took them to Top Pub for a quick meal before he dropped them back to Xander's house. The leap's new Alpha seemed to understand that she and Xander wanted nothing more than to go home so he didn't try to drag out the meal.

After Rocco, she'd promised herself she wouldn't get involved with another man. But she hadn't taken into account that she had a fate-given mate out there waiting for her. As soon as she spent some time with Xander, there was no way could she resist him. Not that she'd tried terribly hard, he was just too irresistible. Whatever higher power designed mates for each other, got her mate spot on. She couldn't have described a more perfect man for her. He was big and strong, but gentle and protective at the same time. Instinctively she knew he'd never hurt her, just as she would never injure him in any way.

Xander said farewell to Dominic and closed the door. They were finally alone. Rachel's heart rate kicked up in anticipation.

"So." She paused to clear her throat. "What's this plan you have?"

He gave her a sly grin as he prowled over to her. "I'm going to get you so turned on, you forget to hold back. Then when you're right on the edge, I'm going to thrust in deep and push us both over."

His voice was deeper and rougher than usual, and she couldn't help but notice the bulge in his jeans. His dirty talk had her clenching her thighs and butt as arousal coursed through her. When he got to her, he didn't miss a step as he picked her up and kept walking. She wrapped her legs around his waist, bringing her core up against his erection. With a moan, she pressed her face against his throat, inhaling deeply and humming in bliss as his woodsy scent filled her head.

He took long strides down the hallway, which had her nipples rubbing against his chest. They were already sensitive, and she shivered with each step he took as they got more stimulation. When he stopped, Rachel lowered her legs to stand, and before she could balance herself, Xander had his mouth on hers. She loved how he kissed her. Full of heat and passion, he drugged her with them until her thoughts swirled and drifted away. All she had in her mind was him and how much she wanted to be in his arms forever.

When they pulled apart, both panting, she locked her gaze with his. "I love you."

His eyes widened a little and a happy grin spread over his face. It was the first time she'd told him and her cheeks began to heat as he stood there still, staring at her. Leaning forward, she ran her hands up under his shirt, lifting it until he took over and pulled it over his head. Mesmerized, she watched how his muscles stretched and bunched with his movements. He was so strong. She ran her palms up his arms, over the curves of his biceps. He could easily break her, yet he didn't. Xander had never once shown her any kind of violence or abuse. Even all those months he watched her in the bar, he was never inappropriate with her, or any other woman.

That first time he'd come into HoHaven, she'd judged him as being just like every other male but now she thought about it, he never watched the girls strip. She'd been able to feel his gaze on her most nights he was there.

"Stop thinking so hard, baby girl. If you don't want to do this tonight, we can wait. We've got forever."

She shook her head. "No. I want this. Want you. A few

things just suddenly became clear."

His arms flexed beneath her touch and her skin tingled at the sensation.

"What things?"

"You only came to HoHaven to watch me, didn't you? When you first came in, I was upset you'd turned out to be like all the other men there. But you weren't, were you?"

His palm cupped her face and he tilted it up until her gaze shifted from his arms and chest to his eyes.

"Damn straight I was there for you. Jake saw your ring that first day in the bar, or I would have dragged you out then and there. It didn't take long to see you weren't happy, so I kept guard on you. Waiting for a chance to talk to you alone, making sure no one tried any shit on you."

She gave him a half smile. "And to take notes on Rocco and his dipshit buddies."

He smirked. "Yeah, I really didn't do too well at my job once I saw you, baby girl. The others were watching the Triggers, I only had eyes for you."

She laughed and decided that was enough of heavy talk of the past.

"Well, I'll have to make sure you stay focused in the future. Can't have you getting distracted."

She stepped back and pulled her shirt over her head as she toed off her shoes. Her breathing sped up as she unclipped her bra. The look in Xander's eyes was so hot, she could feel the heat against her skin. Her bra hadn't hit the floor when he was on her. He hauled her up against him so his face was level with her breasts. She gripped his head as he leaned in and nuzzled his face between them, then he sucked a nipple between his lips, and a spasm deep in her core had her gasping for breath. She arched back as he slid a palm up her spine, his rough skin against hers causing goose bumps to break out. Then with a final nip, he moved to her other breast, licking, sucking and nipping until she was writhing against him.

With a growl, he released her flesh and tossed her backward. With a shriek, she bounced on the mattress, giggling as he attacked her pants and pulled them down her legs. Through hooded lids, she watched Xander strip out of his own jeans. Damn, but that man was one extremely well put together male. And he was all hers, and always would be. She had one hundred percent confidence that he would never, ever cheat on her.

With a smile, she raised her hands to reach for him. "C'mere, babe."

Rachel was the most stunning woman Xander had ever seen. And she was lying spread out before him, naked and waiting. Perfect.

He grabbed a condom and suited up. He wanted to focus on getting her riding the edge of an orgasm. He didn't want to risk her coming back from it while he worried about protection. With one knee on the mattress, he lifted her foot up, pressed a kiss to her ankle bone, then moved up, trailing his lips in a slow slide that had her wriggling around on the bed. He blew gently over the back of her knee and chuckled when she made the most adorable squeaking sound. Hmm, she was ticklish...he could have some fun with that, but not now. Tonight was about claiming and marking what was his.

Gently placing her leg down, spreading her open in the process, he lowered himself until his face was over her core. He inhaled deeply, loving her how her musk mixed with her natural spicy scent. She whimpered and the sound had his dick throbbing with need. Bracing his palms on each of her inner thighs, he used his thumbs to pull her lips open so he could swipe his tongue in deep. He purred as he lapped at her, taking as much cream as she could make. Her hips bucked beneath him and he moved his arms to wrap around her thighs so he could keep her still. He moved between teasing her clit, thrusting his tongue deep, and lapping at her.

Rachel's scent surrounded him, inside and out, and he loved it. He could happily spend a lifetime eating at his mate's core. She still tasted better than anything he'd ever had on his tongue. A tremor ran through her body a moment before she was trying to wriggle away from him.

"It's too much!"

He turned his head to kiss her inner thigh, then sucked hard to leave a mark on her.

"It's perfect, baby girl. Means you're getting close. I can't wait to see you come apart for me. I'll catch you, I promise. Ride the wave and allow yourself to fall over the edge. I'll join you, we'll go over together."

He was already harder than hell, and was sure when she came around him, she'd drag him over with her. He moved up her body, lying over the top of her. He pushed his fist into the pillow to hold his weight off her and leaning to the side, he ran his other palm down her curves until he got to her slick core. He thrust two fingers in deep as he leaned down and took her mouth. With his thumb on her clit between strokes, he had her mewling and writhing beneath him in no time. A sheen of sweat broke out over her body and he shifted to enter her. She was close and he didn't want to miss feeling her coming around his dick.

Gripping his erection, he guided himself into her entrance before he shifted his hand to tease her clit as he flexed his hips and pushed his entire length inside her hot, wet channel. He groaned as he began to pump into her. He kept up working her clit and kissed his way to a nipple, he strained his neck to reach until Rachel cupped herself in her hand and lifted her breast to his mouth. Fuck, she was so perfect for him. This was why he hadn't taken her from behind as was custom with mating. He knew he'd need access to her clit and breasts to keep her riding the edge long enough, she'd tumble over it for him. With him.

He sucked as much of her flesh into his mouth as he could before he sucked hard and fast a few times. Then he scraped his teeth over the tender nipple as he released it. She gasped for air, her body stiffening below him and he thrust into her harder, flicked her clit rougher, and then it happened. Her eyes peeled wide in shock as her core gripped him. With a scream, she threw her head back as she arched up beneath him. Her channel was convulsing around him and he lost his rhythm as he pounded into her, letting his own climax take him.

He had no idea how long it lasted but eventually his mind cleared and holding his still-hard erection within her, he looked down at her sweat slicked face. Her cheeks were flushed red and tears poured down from her eyes. But he wasn't worried he'd hurt her, she was grinning like a fool.

"That was amazing. And overwhelming."

He leaned forward to kiss her but stopped half way. A stinging pain ripped through his hand and he lifted it to see claws form on the fingertips of his right hand.

"Last chance to say no, baby girl. You still want to be my mate?"

Her grin got even wider. "Of course I do!"

Relief and excitement poured through him as he pulled free of his mate's body and rolled her over. He lifted her torso so her back was against his front, with her kneeling in front of him, and palmed the soft flesh just above her right hip bone. Curling his fingers into her flesh, he dragged his claws across her skin. The magic of the marking tingled up his arm and through his entire body until he shuddered behind her. He kept his palm over his mark until the heat from it faded. Then he guided her so she lay on her back once more and grabbed her right wrist gently in his grip so she could watch her own claws grow. Once they were fully out, he placed her hand over his heart, in the area of clean skin he'd left ink free for just this moment.

"Curl your fingers into me, and drag them over. Mark me as yours, Rachel."

She didn't waste time. Within moments he was

shuddering again as the magic of the completed mating rushed through him. While she kept her palm pressed against her mark on him, he looked down at her hip and ran his fingertips lightly over his mark. Four wide scratch marks revealing snow leopard spots arched over her hip bone. She trembled beneath his touch and he had to have her again.

She whimpered as he pulled away from her.

"Hold that thought, baby girl. I'll be right back."

He pawed at the bedside cupboard drawer to grab another condom, then quickly switched over to the new one before he was crawling back over toward his mate's sated body. She spread her legs and held out her arms to him with a serene smile on her face. Within seconds he was thrust deep within her body once more. With one palm resting over his mark that she would now wear forever, he leaned in to kiss her. Her hand came up to cover her mark on him and sparks of awareness shot through his body as he devoured her mouth.

Finally, she was his. Marked and claimed and in his bed where she belonged.

Xander couldn't remember ever being happier.

Epilogue

Rolling his neck, Joel waited for his turn to grab food. As much as he loved the idea their team was going to be a Special Forces Unit, he didn't have the patience for all this training crap. Sawyer had done his best for them, and instead of starting at the bottom and working up the ladder, he'd inserted them at the top. All they had to do was pass the Army testing. The physical stuff wasn't an issue, between shifter instincts and everything Kit had been teaching them. But protocol and structure and the academic side of things was taking way too long to get through.

He'd been dreaming of his girl for eight months. She was a little blonde bombshell who shifted into a sleek, beautiful snow leopard. He couldn't wait to track her down. Not only because he wanted to find her to start their lives together, but for the last few months he'd had a growing sense of unease settle over him. Something was going on with her. Since he'd found out about dream bonding after Jake's funeral, he'd tried to reach out to her but she'd somehow blocked him. Once he was sure he heard a female voice whisper in his mind that he had to stop trying or they'll know.

He didn't know what was going on, but she wasn't being seriously hurt. He'd have felt it if she had, but there was definitely something going on with her.

"You okay?"

Joel turned to face Kit. "Yeah, I'm just getting impatient to hit the road."

"I hear you. I'm about ready to lose my mind. I have that address you boys found, and I can't wait to go see if she's really there."

He winced. Yeah, he wasn't the only one with reasons to rush this training crap. Kit hadn't seen her mother since her dad kicked her out of home at fifteen. Then last year her dad came back with a vengeance. He'd tried to kill Kit and when he'd failed, confessed to her that her mother had left him soon after he'd kicked her out. As a wedding gift, he and his twin had researched the woman and found an address. They'd agreed as a team that as soon as Rachel was rescued, their next mission would be to track the woman down.

That had Joel thinking. Camila Silva, Kit's Mum, lived on a remote property near the Coorong on the coast of South Australia. Joel hadn't ever been there personally but every Australian had seen photos of the area. It was pretty distinctive. There was a wide long strip of sand dunes, a channel of ocean water, then the mainland. He rubbed his fingers over his temples as he closed his eyes and relived his Mate Dreams from the past week.

Initially, his dreams had been all about what she

looked like, but after six months he'd started getting glimpses of other things around her. Things like sand dunes, water and beaches. Could his mate be near Kit's mum?

"You're really starting to worry me. Want me to get Jordan for you?"

Joel shook his head. He didn't want to worry his twin about this shit. He knew his brother had his own issues with his dreams. No sense adding his shit to what the man was already busy worrying about.

"I just put a few things together in my head. I'm fairly certain my mate is down in the Coorong area." He looked up into Kit's eyes. "Near where we located your mum."

"Oh, shit. You're not joking are you? Guess it's a good thing that tomorrow is the last day of our training before we can get going, huh?"

She could say that again. The moment that final test was done, he was out of here. Well, as soon as the team packed their shit and was ready, he'd be heading out to find his mate and kick the ass of anyone dumb enough to be messing with his girl.

Other Fire and Snow books:

More books to come.

Out Now:

Guardian's Heart

Fire and Snow: Book One

The last thing Snow Leopard Shifter Dominic expects to find at an accident scene is his mate, the beautiful Adele. But after four years of dreaming of her, there she is, right in front of him. However, winning the heart of his lonely, grieving mate is no simple task. Just as their relationship begins to heat up, a gravely injured child, Kelly, stumbles into their lives after escaping and fleeing her abuser. Will Dominic and Adele's bond grow stronger as they nurture and protect Kelly? Will their relationship be able to survive all that fate plans on throwing their way?

Noble Guardian

Fire and Snow: Book Two

After watching his older brother win the heart of his mate, Conner White can't wait for his turn. When he finally has his first dream of his mate, he is both relieved that he knows who she is and worried as he hasn't been able to get near her since he caught a glimpse of her at his brother's wedding weeks earlier.

Tina Anderson is beyond miserable. Her mother abandoned her after a life altering injury that left the vibrant gymnast in a wheelchair. Her father has been forced to leave her to go work off shore. She's been left in the care of a harsh bitter woman who is only after her father and will do whatever she deems necessary to take her place in his life. No matter the cost.

Conner and Tina's road to happiness is filled with twists, turns and pot holes, but are they strong enough to pull each other through it all?

Guardian's Shadow

Fire and Snow: Book Three

Jessie loves his life as a carefree rally driver, until a chance meeting with a sexy red haired firefighter changes everything. As a Comet Shifter, Jessie's never met another Snow Leopard shifter before finding Kit, the woman who's haunted his dreams for the past five years.

Kit's one tough female. She's been keeping herself busy protecting those she cares for but deep inside she craves her mate. When her path finally crosses with Jessie sparks fly … and they aren't all the good kind!

Just as they begin to get along, Kit's dark secret is revealed, and it's not only Jessie and Kit that will be put to the test in the aftermath.